Old Testament Legends

being stories out of some of the less–known
apocryphal books of the old testament

Old Testament Legends

being stories out of some of the less-known
apocryphal books of the old testament

M.R. James

ÆGYPAN PRESS

From the edition published by Longmans, Green and Co. in
1913.

Old Testament Legends
A publication of
ÆGYPAN PRESS

www.aegypan.com

Table of Contents

Preface

*I*f you read the title-page of this book — a thing which young persons very seldom do — you will see that it (the book) contains stories taken "out of some of the less-known apocryphal books of the Old Testament." You will very possibly not understand what that means; but if you will read this preface — another thing which young persons do even seldomer than they read a title-page — you will find the best explanation that I can give.

I have to begin by talking about the word apocryphal. The newspapers are fond of saying that a statement made by the Prime Minister (or the leader of the Opposition, according to which side in politics the newspaper takes) is apocryphal. By this, the newspaper means to say that the statement was untrue. Or, you will read that someone obtained money or goods by saying that he possessed large estates abroad; and that the estates turned out to be apocryphal. By this is meant that they did not exist. But when you read of a book being apocryphal, something rather different is meant: either that it is "spurious," i.e. that it pretends to be written by someone who did not write it; or that what is in it is fabulous and untrue, like the stories of King Arthur; or both.

Now this word apocryphal is specially used, and perhaps most often used, in connection with the Bible. Probably you have at least heard of something called "the Apocrypha," even if you have not read it, and even if you have mixed it up in your mind with another word, Apocalypse, which has nothing whatever to do with it. Well, what is "the Apocrypha?" It is to be found in many Bibles, bound up between the Old and the New Testaments. It is a set of books, looking just like the other books of the Bible, with chapters and verses. Some of it is read in church as weekday lessons in the months of October and November, as you may see by looking at the Table of Lessons in any Prayer Book. Now, are all these books of "the Apocrypha" fabulous or spurious? No. Some of them are. The Second Book of Esdras (that is, Ezra) was not written by Ezra; The Book of Baruch (the companion of the prophet Jeremiah) was not written by Baruch; The Wisdom of Solomon was not written by Solomon. These and some others are spurious. Also, the books of Tobit and of Judith are fabulous stories. On the other hand, the book Ecclesiasticus was really written by Sirach (who is mentioned in the Preface), and The First Book of Maccabees is a true and valuable history.

Then why, if apocryphal means fabulous or spurious, or both, are these books, some of which are true and genuine, lumped all together and called "Apocrypha?" I am sorry to disappoint you, but I cannot go through the whole history. It is long, it is difficult, and though it interests me, I am inclined to think it would not interest you unless I spread it over a great many pages, and filled it out with stories; and for this I have no time. Let me tell you what strikes me as being the important thing to bear in mind. Nearly all of these books have been at some time or another read in church and treated as Scripture. Nearly all of them are now treated as Scripture by the Roman Church, but not by most of the Protestant, or Reformed, Churches. They are on the borderland of the Bible. From having been so long kept together in a group by themselves, they have come to be thought of as being all of one uniform kind. But they are not so; they are of very different sorts and merits.

Let us keep the old name for them and call them "the Apocrypha." It will be convenient to do so, because I have now to speak of other apocryphal books, which have never been bound up in our Bibles, but in older times, before Bibles were printed, were (some of them at least) read in churches and thought to be sacred books. There are a great many of these: perhaps, if they were all put together, they would make up a volume as large as the Old Testament itself; but at present there is no book in which they are all printed together. Some are stories, others are visions like those in the Revelation of St. John, others are psalms and prophecies. But all of them, I think, may fairly be called either fabulous or spurious, or both.

I can give you an example from the Bible itself to show that there were such books as long ago as the times of the Apostles, and that they were read and valued. In the 9th verse of the Epistle of Jude, you read something very curious about Satan contending with Michael about the body of Moses. Ancient writers whom we may trust tell us that this is taken from a book called The Assumption of Moses (that is, the story of Moses being taken up out of this world at the end of his life).

We have pieces of this book still, but we have not got the whole story of the dispute between Satan and Michael. However, we know that it was represented as having taken place when Michael and the other angels were burying the body of Moses among the mountains in a place which was kept secret from all men, and that Satan said that though the soul of Moses might belong to God, the body belonged to him; and, moreover, that Moses was a murderer, because, long before, he had killed an Egyptian (as we read in Exodus ii. 12); whereupon Michael answered Satan in the words, "The Lord rebuke thee," and Satan fled. That is one example. Another is in the 14th verse of the same Epistle, where it is said that Enoch, the seventh from Adam, prophesied of the coming of the Lord to judge sinners. This verse is taken out of a long book of prophecies and visions called The Book of Enoch, which still exists, and we may read the very words in it.

In this present book, I am only concerned with the apocryphal stories; with the prophecies and visions and psalms I have nothing to do. Now, how and why did the stories come to be written?

It is likely enough that after reading some history in the Bible you may have wondered whether there was anything more to be known about the people of whom it told you. You would have liked to find out what happened to Adam, or Joseph, or David, besides the things which are written in the Bible. It was just so in ancient times — the times when our Lord was on earth, and even long before that. The Jews naturally thought a great deal about the people who are mentioned in the Old Testament; and just as there are a great many stories about the heroes of English history — such as that of King Alfred and the cakes — which, we are told now, are not true, so stories grew up about the great men of the Bible. Perhaps they were invented, some of them, in answer to questions which had been asked. Some of them were certainly made up in order to explain parts of the Bible which were difficult to understand. I will give an example of this. In the Book of Genesis (iv. 23, 24) you are told how the patriarch Lamech spoke to his wives and said, "I have slain a man to my wounding, and a young man to my hurt." Nothing is said in explanation of this; we are not told whom Lamech had killed. So a story was made up — no one knows when — which gives this explanation: Lamech was blind, and he used to amuse himself by shooting birds and beasts with bow and arrow. When he went out shooting, he used to take with him his young nephew Tubal; and Tubal used to spy the game for him and guide his hands that he might aim his arrow right. One day, when they were out together, Tubal saw, as he thought, a beast moving in the thicket; and he told Lamech, and made him aim at it, and Lamech's arrow smote the beast and killed it. But when Tubal ran to see what kind of beast it was, he found that it was not a wild beast at all. It was his ancestor Gain. For after Gain had killed Abel, and God had pronounced a curse upon him, he wandered about the earth, never able to remain in one place; and a great horn grew out of his head, and his body was covered with hair; so that Tubal, seeing him in the distance among the trunks of the trees and the brushwood, was deceived, and mistook him for a beast of chase. But when Tubal saw what had happened, he was terrified, and ran back to Lamech, crying out, "You have slain our forefather Cain!" And Lamech also was struck with horror, and raised his hands and smote them together with a mighty blow. And in so doing he struck the head of Tubal with his full strength, and Tubal fell down dead. Then Lamech returned to his house, and spoke to his wives the words that are written in the Book of Genesis. This story, a very ancient one, as I said, was invented by the Jews to explain the difficult passage in Genesis; and the early Christian writers learnt it from the Jews, and it passed into many commentaries which were written in later times; so that you may still see representations of it carved in stone in churches, both in England and elsewhere. In England it may be seen on the inside of the stone roof of Norwich Cathedral, and on the west front of Wells Cathedral; but you have to look carefully before you can find it.

There are other stories which pretend to explain texts that do not seem so difficult. For instance, in the 18th Psalm there is a verse, "Thou hast made room enough under me for to go." And about this there is a long tale of how King David went to fight the giant Ishbibenob, and was nearly killed by him; for the giant took David and cast him to the ground, and put a heavy wine-press upon him, which would have crushed him, but that the earth beneath him suddenly became soft and yielded room for his body, and thus room was made under him.

Then again, there are others which are like parables.

At this point I will put in two short stories of the parable-kind, neither of which I think you are likely to have seen. One of them is certainly taken from an apocryphal book which is lost; and the other I suspect to have been taken either from the same book or from one like it.

First I will tell the one about the source of which I am not certain.

In the days of King Hezekiah there was in Israel a rich man who was a miser and gave nothing to the poor. But one day it happened that he took up the book of the proverbs of King Solomon; and his eye fell upon the place where it is said, "He that hath pity upon the poor, lendeth unto the Lord; and look what he layeth out, it shall be paid him again." "So," thought he to himself, "this is a good security!" And forthwith he sold all that he had, and distributed the price among the poor, keeping for himself only two pieces of money. But, to his disappointment, he did not only become poor himself by this means, but he remained poor. The money he had given away did not come back, and no one else would give him any. So he was reduced to despair, and said, "I will go straight to Jerusalem, and demand of God why He has deceived me, and induced me to give away all my possessions by promises that are false." And he set forth. And on his way, not far from Jerusalem, he saw two men fighting, and said to them, "Brethren, what is your quarrel?" And one said, "We were journeying together, and I saw a shining stone lying in the road, and pointed it out to this man; and because he was swifter on his feet than I, he got to it first. And now he says he will keep it for himself, but I say it belongs to me, for I saw it first." Then said the traveler, "What is the value of the stone?" They said, "We do not know." And he said, "Will you take these two pieces of money for it and let me have it?" And to this they consented. So when the man got to Jerusalem, he took the stone to a jeweler and showed it to him; and no sooner had the jeweler seen it than he fell on his face and gave thanks to God. And then he said to the man, "Where did you find this? For three whole years all Jerusalem has been ransacked for this stone. Go quickly to the High Priest and give it to him, and see what he will give you!" At the same hour there came an angel to the High Priest, and said to him, "Within a few moments there will come to you a man bringing the gem which three years ago was lost out of the breastplate of Aaron the priest. Receive it at his hands, and give him for it a great sum of gold; and when you have given it, smite him lightly upon the cheek and say, 'Be not distrustful in thy heart, and slow to believe the word which says, 'He that hath pity upon the poor, lendeth unto the Lord.' For thus saith the Lord, 'Have I not now in this present world repaid thee many times over that which thou didst lend to Me? And, if thou have faith, thou shalt in the world to come receive a recompense yet many times greater than this.'" And when the man came, the High Priest did and said as he had been commanded; and the man's heart was moved, and he left in the temple all that great sum which had been given him, and for the rest of his life put his whole trust in the promises of God.

The other short story is taken out of an apocryphal book under the name of the prophet Ezekiel, and is a parable of the soul and the body of man at the day of judgment.

There was a certain king, it says, who made a marriage feast for his eldest son, and invited all his soldiers to his palace to share it. Now every one of his subjects was a soldier and served in his army, except only two, one of whom was blind and the other lame; and these two were not invited to the feast, but remained in their huts — which were near to one another — very angry and disappointed. After a while the blind man called to the lame man, "It is a shame that we are not sitting down to the feast along with the rest! I should like to treat the king as ill as he has treated us." "How can we?" said the lame man. "You know his garden," said the other; "let us go and spoil it!" "All very well," said the lame man, "but how are we to get there? I cannot walk." "Neither can I see; but we will contrive a way." So they devised a plan. The lame man plucked the grass that he could reach, and plaited it into a string, and threw one end to the blind man, who guided himself by it to the lame man. Then he took the lame man on his back, and carried him to the king's garden, and there they did all the mischief they could, trampling down and tearing up plants and flowers; and they went back to their houses and remained there. When the rest of the people came out from the banquet into the garden, they were appalled at the sight of the damage, and were much perplexed, saying, "Were not all the soldiers of the king bidden to the feast? and is not every man in the kingdom a soldier? Whence then are these tracks in the garden, and who has wrought this mischief?" After a while the king bethought him of the blind and the lame man; they were brought before him, and he said to the blind man, "Have you been into my garden?" He answered, "Alas, sire! you see my infirmity, and that I have no eyes wherewith to find my way!" Then said the king to the lame man, "And you, have you been into my garden?" And he answered, "Surely my lord has forgotten my infirmity; it cannot be that he desires to hurt my feelings by mocking me!" So the king was perplexed, and went apart to consider how the two could have contrived the business — for he was sure that they were guilty. At last a thought came to him, and he set the lame man on the blind man's shoulders, and scourged them both together. Then indeed did they cry out, and the lame said to the blind, "Did you not lend me your feet to take me to the king's garden?" And the blind to the lame, "Did you not lend me your eyes to show me the way?" And in like manner at the judgment the soul will say to the body, "I could not have sinned if you had not given me the limbs with which I did evil." And the body to the soul, "But it was you who thought of the evil which I carried out." Thus one will try to throw the blame on the other; but is either of them free from guilt?

Others of these apocryphal books are designed to show how important some special virtue, or how dangerous some particular sin, may be. Thus, there is a book called The Testaments (or Last Words) of the Twelve Patriarchs, in which each of the twelve sons of

Jacob, when he comes to die, calls his children to him and tells them about his own life, and warns them against his own besetting sin, or shows how he has been helped by practicing some good habit: Simeon speaks about envy, Issachar about simplicity, Zebulun about kindness, and so on. And many others there are which are merely, one would say, meant to tell us more about the lives and deaths of the great men of the old times than we can learn from the Bible.

Perhaps I have now said enough to show of what sort the tales are that are told in this book — some of them told for the first time in English. They are not true, but they are very old; some of them, I think, are beautiful, and all of them seem to me interesting. In case anyone should wish to know more about them, I will put down here the names of the books from which I have taken them.

The first part of the story of Adam is shortened from Mr. S. G. Malan's translation of The Book of Adam and Eve, and from Dillmann's German translation of the same (Das christliche Adambuch des Morgenlandes). The second part is from the Greek Revelation of Moses (in Tischendorf's Apocalypses Apocryphae), and from the Latin Life of Adam, edited by W. Meyer.

The first part of the story of Abraham is from The Apocalypse of Abraham, translated from Slavonic by Professor N. Bonwetsch; the second part is from The Testament of Abraham, edited by me in Texts and Studies.

The story of Aseneth is from the Greek History of Aseneth, edited by Batiffol in Studia Patristica.

The story of Job is taken from The Testament of Job in my Apocrypha Anecdota (ii).

That of Solomon is from The Testament of Solomon as printed by Migne at the end of the works of Michael Psellus.

That of Baruch from The Rest of the Words of Baruch, edited by Dr. J. Rendel Harris.

That of Ahikar principally from the French edition by the Abbé F. Nau, with some few touches borrowed from that by Dr. J. Rendel Harris.

One last word. Not all of the stories in this book are equally old. The oldest is most likely that of Ahikar. Lately some pieces of it have been discovered in Egypt in a very ancient copy. Next, probably, comes the second part of the story of Adam. In each of the others there are some parts which are derived from early Jewish tales, but the books in which we have them now were put into their present shape by Christians. Still, there is not one that is less than fifteen hundred years old.

Adam

*W*hen Adam and Eve were driven out of the Garden of Eden, they were as helpless as little children. They knew nothing of day or night, heat or cold; they could not kindle a fire to warm themselves, nor till the ground to grow food. They had as yet no clothes to wear and no shelter against rain or sun. As long as they were in the garden, it was always light and warm, and their bodies were so fashioned that they had no need of food or sleep or of protection against the burning of the sun; but since they had eaten of the Tree of Knowledge, they had become like us. Moreover, all the beasts and birds were friendly with them; but now they knew that it was not so, and that they had no defense if any fierce animal chose to attack them; and, more than all, they knew that they had a cruel enemy lying in wait for them outside the garden, even Satan, who had hated them from the first, and had brought about their fall by means of the serpent. And so it was that when they came out of the gate of the garden and saw the earth stretched out before them, covered with rocks and sand, and found themselves in a strange land where there was no one to guide them, they fell down on their faces, and became as dead, because of the misery and sorrow which they felt. But God looked upon them and sent His Word to raise them up and comfort them; and showed them a place not very far from the garden where there was a cave; and told them that they were to live there. Now this was the cave which was afterwards called the Gave of Treasures.

When first they entered into the cave, they did nothing but weep and lament: not only because they had lost the garden, but also because for the first time the sky was hidden from them by the roof of the cave; for as yet they had never been in anyplace where they could not see it. But when the sun set and there was darkness outside the cave as well as inside, they were frightened beyond measure; for they said, "It is because of what we have done: the light is gone out of the heavens, and will come back no more." Then the Word of God spake to them and said, "Be comforted; it is only so for a few hours, and the light will return to you." And they remained praying and weeping in the cave until the darkness began to grow less. After that the sun rose, and Adam went to the mouth of the cave, and it shone full upon him, and he felt the burning heat of it on his body for the first time, and thought that it was God who had come to afflict and punish him; and he beat upon his breast and prayed for mercy. But God said, "This sun is not God; it is created to give light to the world, and every day it will rise in like manner, and travel over the heavens and set, as you have seen it. *I* am God, who comforted you in the night."

Then Adam and Eve took courage, and came out of the cave, and thought they would go towards the garden; and when they came near to the gate by which they had been driven out of it, they met the serpent. Now before it tempted Eve and became accursed, the serpent had been the most beautiful of all the creatures.

Its head was of all the colors of the most beautiful jewels; it had eyes like emeralds, and a melodious voice; it had slender and graceful legs, and it fed on perfumed flowers and delicious fruits. Now it was loathsome to look upon; it wriggled on its belly in the dust, and all creatures spurned and hated it. And when it saw Eve it was enraged to think of the curse that had come upon it through her, and it raised itself up and darted at her, and its eyes became blood-red with anger. Then Adam, who had nothing in his hand wherewith to defend Eve, ran and caught it by the tail, but it turned upon him and coiled about him and Eve with its body and began to crush them; and it said, "It is because of you that I am compelled to trail in the dust and have lost my beauty." And they cried out for fear. But God sent an angel who caught hold of the serpent and loosed them, and smote the serpent with dumbness, so that thereafter it could only hiss. And a great wind came and took it up, and cast it away upon the seashore of India.

And when Adam and Eve had a little recovered themselves from their fear, they went on towards the garden; but at the gate of it there stood a great cherub holding a sword of fire; and when they were able to look upon his face, they saw that he was angry and that he frowned upon them, and raised his sword as if he would smite them with it; but he said nothing. So they were in great fear, and turned from him and went back in great sorrow of heart, wandering they knew not whither, until they found themselves standing on the top of a rock, and before their feet was a precipice. And Adam was so miserable that he desired to live no longer; and he cast himself down from the top of the rock, and lay on the ground below without moving; and Eve thought that he was dead, and said, "I will not live after him; it is through my fault that all these evils

have come upon him." And she also threw herself
down from the top of the rock; but though both of
them were torn and bruised, they were not wounded
to death. And after a long time they came to themselves.

Then they bethought them that they had done wrong
in trying to put an end to their own lives before it
pleased God to set them free from this world. Therefore
Adam took stones and piled them up in the shape of
an altar, and then they gathered leaves from the trees
and wiped off the blood that had been spilt upon the
face of the rock, and gathered up the dust that was
mingled with their blood and laid it upon the altar,
and prayed to God to forgive their trespass. And this
was the first offering that they made to God. And God
looked upon them with pity and forgave them, and
said, "As you have shed your blood, so after five
thousand and five hundred years have passed will I
take your flesh upon Me and shed My blood for you
and for your children; and it shall have power to
quench the flame of the sword which is in the hand of
the angel, and you shall enter again into the garden,
and dwell there until the time when I shall make a new
heaven and a new earth."

But when Satan saw that God had pity upon Adam
and Eve and accepted their humble offering — for he
was all this time keeping watch to see what would
become of them — he was filled with dismay and hate,
and began to contrive means by which he might lead
them astray and put an end to them; for he thought,
"If these creatures were destroyed, the earth would
remain to me and to my hosts, and I should reign over
it alone." He called therefore for some of his host, and
made them appear like angels of light. And when they
were all disguised in this fashion, they rose into the air
and flew towards the cave, from which Adam and Eve

were just coming out, meaning to go once again towards the garden. When they caught sight of these bright ones in the air, they stopped and raised their hands towards them, thinking that they were angels coming to them with a message. Satan called to Adam, "Adam, we are angels come from God; He has sent us to bring you to the lake of pure water that is on the north side of Eden, that you may wash yourselves in it and be cleansed from your sin, and return once more to the garden. Come therefore and follow us." And they turned and began flying towards the north; but Adam and Eve were glad beyond measure, and followed the troop of angels as quickly as they could, till they came to the mountain on the north side of Eden which overhung the lake. Then Satan lighted on the ground, and guided them to the top of the mountain, which was very steep. And when they were at the summit, they stood for a while and looked down upon the waters of the lake; and while they were doing so, Satan vanished away silently, and all his host with him; so that when Adam and Eve looked round, they found themselves left alone and in great peril. And they saw that they had been brought into this danger by Satan, and that he had deceived them once again. And they cried aloud for help.

Then God had pity on them, and commanded the angels Sariel and Salathiel to bear them in their arms and carry them back to their cave. And when they were come there, Adam prayed to God that, if they might not be permitted to go into the garden anymore, He would at least give them something for a remembrance of it to comfort them. So God commanded the archangel Michael to go as far as the Sea of India, and fetch thence some gold, and dip it in the water that flows from under the Tree of Life, and give it to Adam. Likewise He commanded Gabriel to speak to the cherub that kept the gate of the garden, and go in and fetch some frankincense; and Raphael to bring myrrh also from the garden. And they did so. And Michael brought seventy rods of gold, and Gabriel twelve pounds weight of frankincense, and Raphael three pounds of myrrh; and these were all laid up in the cave where Adam and Eve lived: wherefore it was called the Gave of Treasures. And when the appointed time was fulfilled, and the Word took upon Him the flesh of the sons of Adam, three kings came from the East to do Him honor, and offered to Him that same gold and frankincense and myrrh, which had come down to them through many generations.

After some days, Adam and Eve made a vow that they would go, one of them to the river Tigris and the other to the river Euphrates, and would wade into the water up to the neck, and stand there for forty whole days and nights, praying earnestly that they might be forgiven; for even yet they went on hoping that, if they accomplished some great act of repentance, they might be permitted to return into Eden. They separated, therefore, and stood in the water of the river, fasting and praying. But Satan suspected that they had made such a vow, and it frightened him, for he did not feel sure that God would not change His purpose and forgive them; and he said to himself, "I will take care that they shall not keep their vow." Accordingly, on the thirty-fifth day, as Eve stood praying in the water, she heard a voice as of an angel praising God, and she looked and saw one in bright raiment coming to her, and he called to her and said, "God has forgiven Adam! All is well. I have just now brought the good tidings to Adam, and he bade me come and tell you; and lest you should doubt of the truth, he said, 'Remind her of the sign which was given to us in the cave: how the angels brought the gold and laid it on the south side, and the incense on the east, and the myrrh on the west."' Then Eve was sure that the messenger spoke true, and she rejoiced greatly, and came, as well as she could, out of the water, and followed him. But when they came in sight of the river Euphrates, she saw Adam still standing in the water praying, and she knew that she had been deceived; and at that moment Satan vanished away, and Eve fell upon the ground, for she was stiff with the cold, and weak with fasting. As for Adam, when he saw her, he cried out and smote upon his breast, and sank down into the water, and would have perished but that God sent His angel and drew him up out of the water. And he showed Adam that he could not by these means gain admittance to the garden before the time appointed was fulfilled.

After these things God showed Adam and Eve the things that were necessary for their life. For as yet they had eaten nothing since they came out of the garden; because the food which they had when they were there was heavenly food, and it sustained them through all these many days. Neither had they any clothes. Therefore God told them to go to the seashore, and there they should find the skins of some sheep whose flesh had been devoured by lions, and these skins they should take and make them into raiment. But Satan heard the words of God, and immediately went to the place where the skins were, with intent to throw them into the sea, or burn them with fire; only, just as he was about to seize them, God spake a word, and Satan was bound there immovable, in his own hideous form. And when Adam and Eve came to the place, they saw him crouching beside the skins; and they were afraid at the horrible look of him. Then the Word came to them, saying, "This is he who promised to make you as gods. What have you gained, think you, by hearkening to his words?" And Satan was cowed, and fled away in shame.

Adam and Eve therefore took the sheep-skins, and there came an angel who showed them how to sew them together with palm-thorns and sinews, and they made them into raiment.

Again, God showed them a land where corn was growing, and told them how they might use it for bread; for it was ripe, and they gathered the ears and made an offering of the first ears. And Satan came and burned part of the corn; but the angels drove him away.

Many other times also did Satan try to destroy Adam and Eve, coming to them disguised as an angel and enticing them into the wilderness; and again, when they were sleeping on the side of a mountain outside their cave, he loosened a great rock above them that it might fall and crush them; but the angels of God caught it and fixed it like a roof over the heads of Adam and Eve, and when they awoke they were astonished. And once he fell upon Adam and smote him in the side with a sharp stone so that he almost slew him. Nevertheless, in all these perils Adam and Eve put their trust in God, and He protected them and healed them. And after a time Satan perceived that he would not be able to destroy them by injuring their bodies, and that they would not listen to him when he tempted them to disobey God. So Satan's war against Adam was defeated.

This is the first part of the story of Adam, as it is told in an old book called The Conflict of Adam and Eve. It is only part of the story; I have left out a great deal. The second part of the story is taken from a Greek book called The Revelation of Moses, and a Latin one called The Life of Adam and Eve. It tells how Adam died and was buried.

The Death of Adam and Eve

*A*dam lived for 930 years; and there were born to him thirty sons and thirty daughters. And when he was 930 years old he fell sick, and sent for all his children, and for their children also, saying, "Come and let me see you before I die." They all gathered together therefore at the door of his dwelling, saving Gain, who was a wanderer upon the face of the earth; but Seth was the eldest of those that came, and he was the most beloved son of Adam and Eve.

And Seth said to his father, "Father, what is the matter with you?" And Adam answered, "Great pain and sickness is upon me." And his children said, "What mean you by pain and sickness?" For as yet no one had died upon the earth except Abel, whom Gain slew. Then said Seth, "Father, is it because you long after the garden and desire the fruit of it? If it be so, command me, and I will go to the gate, and cast dust upon my head, and weep and pray; and God will send His angel, and it may be He will suffer me to bring you some of the fruit of the garden, and you shall eat it and recover." Eve also wept and said, "My lord Adam, give me the half of your disease, and let me bear it for you; because it is through my fault that this evil has come upon you." Then said Adam, "I will tell you what you shall do, even you and my son Seth: you shall go to the garden and pray there as you have said, and ask the angel to give me some of the oil of mercy that flows from the Tree of Life, and bring it to me that I may anoint my body with it, and be eased from my pain."

So Eve and Seth departed and went towards the garden; and as they were going through the woods, a wild beast leaped out and attacked Seth. And Eve was terrified and cried out, "Alas! alas! what will become of me at the last day? Surely all that have done evil will curse me, saying, 'Woe unto Eve, because she kept not the commandment of God!'" And she cried out upon the wild beast, "How wast thou not afraid to fight against the image of God? How is thy mouth opened against Him? Dost thou not remember that God put thee in subjection to us?" And the beast spake with a man's voice and said, "What have we to do with thy weeping and complaints? How was it that thy mouth was opened to eat of the fruit? Accuse me not, lest I begin to accuse thee." Then said Seth to the beast, "Shut thy mouth: be silent: dare not to touch the image of God." And the beast answered, "Thee will I obey, O Seth." And it fled and left him wounded, and went back to its den.

So Eve and Seth went on to the garden and wept before the gate, beseeching God to send them the oil of mercy for Adam. And God sent Michael the arch-angel to them, who said, "Seth, thou man of God, weary not thyself with making supplication for the oil of mercy, for it cannot be given to thee now. But when the times are fulfilled, then shall come One who shall anoint thy father with that oil, and he shall rise up and return to the garden, he and all his seed; and the evil heart shall be taken from them, and a new heart shall be given them to understand that which is good, and God shall dwell in the midst of them, and they shall be His people. But now go back to thy father, for his end is near, even within three days, and tell him these words; and watch what shall come to pass when he is taken from thee." They returned therefore to Adam, and told him; and he groaned and said, "Alas! O Eve, what is this that thou hast done, to bring upon us the dominion of death? Now therefore call together our children and our children's children, and tell them concerning our sin, from first to last." So, when they were assembled, Eve spoke to them, and told them the whole story of how Satan came to the serpent and taunted it for paying homage to Adam and Eve, forasmuch as they were neither so beautiful nor so wise as itself; and he persuaded the serpent to let him speak through its mouth; and at the hour when the angels go up to the heavens to worship God, the serpent slipped over the wall and found Eve by the Tree of Knowledge; and of what happened after that, until the time when they were cast out of the garden. And when she ceased speaking, her children departed.

Then she went in to Adam, and said to him,

"How can I live when you are dead? and how long will it be before I also die? Tell me." Adam answered, "Trouble not yourself; for you will not tarry long after me, and I believe that the same grave will hold both of us. But now, when I die, leave me alone, and let no one touch me until the will of God is made known concerning me. For I am sure that God will not forget me, but will visit the creature which His hands have made. Now therefore go and pray to Him until I give up my spirit to Him that gave it; for we know not how we shall meet Him, whether He will yet be wroth with us, or whether He will turn and have mercy upon us."

She went out therefore and fell upon the ground and prayed a long time.

And at last the Angel of Mankind came to her and said, "Rise up, Eve; for Adam thy husband is departing out of this life, and is going to meet Him that made him."

Eve therefore arose and looked up into the sky; and she saw a chariot of light coming, drawn by four shining eagles, and angels on either side escorting the chariot. And when it came above the place where our father Adam lay, it stayed. And the angels came bearing censers, and they stood about it and lighted their censers, and the smoke of the incense rose up and hid the firmament; and the angels bowed and worshipped, saying, "Holy One, have mercy, for he is Thine image and the work of Thy hands."

Also Eve beheld two great and fearful ones standing in the heavens, and she was afraid and called upon Seth, saying, "Rise up, O Seth, and come to me, and behold that which no eye of man hath looked upon." So he came to her, and she said, "Seest thou the seven heavens open, and thy father Adam lying upon his face and the holy angels interceding for him?" She said, moreover, "Who are the two dark ones that stand praying for thy father?" And Seth answered, "They are the Sun and the Moon, who are entreating the Most High for my father Adam." And Eve said, "Where then is their light, and why is their aspect black?" And he said, "They cannot shine in the presence of the Light of all things: therefore is their light departed from them."

Now as Seth was speaking to his mother, behold, the angels blew with the trumpets, and fell on their faces, and cried with a loud voice, "Blessed be the glory of the Lord over all His works; for He hath had compassion upon Adam, the work of His hands." Then came one of the Seraphim, having six wings, and caught up the soul of Adam and bare it to the lake of pure water which is on the north side of Eden, and washed it before the face of God. And the Most High commanded him to deliver it unto Michael the archangel, that he should bear it into Paradise until the day of the visitation of all things.

After that the holy archangel entreated the Most High concerning the body of Adam. And God commanded all the angels to come before Him, everyone in his order; and they gathered themselves together, bearing censers and trumpets and vials full of odors. And the Lord of Hosts went up, and the great winds before Him, and the Cherubim flying upon the winds, and the angels of heaven round about Him. And they bore up the body of Adam and carried it into the garden. And all the trees of the garden bowed and swayed and gave forth their odors. And because of the greatness of that sight, and of the sweetness of the odors of Paradise, all the sons of Adam, and all that were on the earth, were cast into a deep sleep, saving Seth only.

Now as the body of Adam lay in Paradise, God said, "O Adam, why didst thou transgress My commandment? For if thou hadst kept it, they that persecute thee would not have rejoiced against thee. Nevertheless I say unto thee, that hereafter I will turn their joy into sorrow, and thy sorrow into joy."

Then the angels brought shrouds of silk and fine linen, and God commanded Michael, Gabriel, Uriel, and Raphael, and they wrapped up the body of Adam therein, and anointed it with sweet odors. And the Lord said, "Bring hither also the body of Abel." For since the day when Gain slew him, the body of Abel had not been buried: because Gain often sought to hide it, but the earth would not receive it, until the dust that was first taken out of her and made into a body, that is, the body of Adam, should be restored to her.

So the body of Abel was brought and wrapped in grave-clothes like that of Adam; and they were both of them buried in the place from which God took the dust when He formed Adam at the first, and the angels dug the grave and covered it in.

And when this was done, God called to the body, saying, "Adam, Adam!" And the body answered, "Here am I, Lord." And the Lord said, "I said unto thee, 'Dust thou art and unto dust shalt thou return.' Behold now I promise thee that in the last days I will raise thee up yet again out of the dust, even thee and all thy seed with thee." And God sealed the tomb that no man should touch it until six days were fulfilled, and the rib which was taken out of Adam should be given back to him.

After these things Eve awoke out of her sleep, and was troubled because she knew not what had become of the body of Adam; and she prayed, saying, "Lord, as Thou didst make me out of the flesh of Adam, and as I was with him in the garden, and after we were cast out I was never parted from him, so now, I beseech thee, suffer me to be buried with him, and let no man part us asunder." And on the seventh day after the death of Adam, Eve was thus praying; and when she had ended her prayer, she looked up into heaven and smote her breast and said, "Lord God of all things, receive my spirit." And so she gave up her soul to God.

And immediately the angels came and took her body, and buried it in the place where the bodies of Adam and Abel were laid.

Abraham

Abraham was the son of Terah, and Terah was a maker of idols which he sold to the people round about him. Now this is the story of how Abraham came to believe in the true God; and in the ancient book the story is put into the mouth of Abraham himself, and he tells it in this way:

I was troubled in my mind because I desired to know who was in truth the strongest of all the Gods. And one day when I was attending to the gods of my father Terah, gods of wood and stone, gold and silver, iron and brass, I went into the temple where they stood, and found that one of them, the god named Marumath, who was carved out of stone, had fallen over and was lying at the feet of the god Zucheus. When I saw that, I was alarmed, and thought that I should never be able to put him back in his place by myself, because he was so heavy; so I went and told my father, and he came, and the two of us could hardly manage to move him; but as we were doing so, the head of the god broke off in my hands. At that my father said, "Abraham," and I said, "Here am I, bring me the chisels out of the house." And when I had done so, he fashioned another

Marumath out of stone, without a head, and fixed the head that had come off the first Marumath upon it; and the rest of the old Marumath he broke in pieces.

After that he made five more gods, and bade me take them and sell them in the streets of the city; and I saddled the ass, and put them upon it, and went to the river to sell them; and there I found merchants coming from Fandana in Syria with camels, on their way to Egypt to bring papyrus from the Nile. And as I was talking with them one of their camels belched, and the donkey took fright and ran off, and the gods fell off its back, and three of them were broken, and only two remained whole. But when the Syrians saw what had happened, they said, "Why did you not tell us that you had gods to sell? We might have bought them before the donkey took fright, and they would not have been destroyed; at least we will take the gods that remain, and pay you the price of them all." And they did so; and the broken gods I cast into the river Gur, and they sank and were seen no more.

But as I returned home, I was bewildered and divided in my mind. I said to myself, "What an evil trade is this that my father practices! Is not he in truth the god of his own gods which he makes with his chisels and lathes and his skill? Ought they not rather to worship him than he them? Surely it is all deceit. Look at Marumath, who fell and could not get up again, and these five other gods which could not punish the donkey for running away with them, nor keep themselves from being broken and thrown into the river."

And as I was thinking of all these things, I arrived at my father's house. Then I gave the ass his hay and water, and went in and gave the price of the gods to my father Terah, and he was pleased and said, "Blessed be thou of my gods: my labor has not been in vain." But I said, "It is rather thou, father, that givest blessing to the gods, for thou art their god; their own blessing is vain and their help is naught: if they cannot help themselves, how should they help thee or bless me?" But he was very angry with me for speaking lightly of his gods.

Then I went out of the house, and after a while my father called me and said, "Gather up the chips of the fig-wood wherewith I was making gods before you came in, and see about preparing dinner."

And as I was doing so, I found a little god lying among the straw and the rubbish, and on his forehead was written: "The god Barisat." So I kept him, and did not tell my father; and when I had kindled the fire to cook the dinner, and was going out to fetch the food, I set Barisat down in front of the fire and said to him, "Barisat, take care that the fire does not go out before I come back; and if it does, blow upon it and revive it." Then I went out and did my errand, and when I returned I found Barisat fallen over backwards, and his feet were in the fire and were badly burned; and I laughed to myself and said, "You are in truth a good fireman and cook, Barisat." Just then the fire caught upon his body and burned him all up.

When the time was come, I brought food to my father and he ate, and I gave him wine and milk and he drank, and rejoiced and praised his god Marumath; and I said, "Father, you should not praise Marumath, but rather Barisat, for he has done more for you: he has thrown himself into the fire to cook your dinner." "And where is he now?" said my father. "He has been burned to ashes," I said, "in the heat of the fire, and nothing but dust is left of him." And my father said, "Great is the strength of Barisat! I will make another one today, and he shall prepare my food for me tomorrow." Now when I heard my father say these words, I laughed in myself, and yet I was troubled and angry in my soul. And at last I answered and said, "Whichever of these things you honor as a god, it is folly. The god Zucheus, who is the god of my brother Nahor, is more honorable than your god Marumath, for he is adorned with gold finely wrought, and when he is old he will be fashioned over again; but if Marumath is broken or injured he will not be renewed, for he is only of stone. And again the god Joauv, who stands next to Zucheus, is more honorable than Barisat, for he is covered with silver; but as for Barisat, you made him yourself with your axe, and, look, he is fallen upon the earth, and the fashion of his likeness is destroyed, and he is burned to ashes, and you say, 'Today I will make another, and he shall prepare my food tomorrow.'

"But I say to you, my father, the fire is mightier than all your gods of gold and silver and stone and wood, for it can devour them all. Yet I call not the fire god, for it is weaker than the water which can subdue it. Yet again I call not the water god, for the earth swallows it up. Neither call I the earth god, for it is subject to men that till it, and to the sun that gives light to it. Neither call I the sun god, for it is overcome by the darkness of night. But I say that there is one true God who hath made all these things; who hath made the heavens blue, and the sun golden, and the moon and stars white and shining, and hath raised up the earth from among the waters, and breathed into thee the breath of life, and hath sought me out in the trouble of my soul; and would that He might reveal Himself unto us!"

And as I was speaking these words to my father in the court of his house, there came from heaven the voice of a Mighty One speaking out of a cloud of fire, and said, "Abraham, Abraham!" And I said, "Behold, here am I!" And He said, "In the thought of thy heart thou seekest after the God of Gods and the Maker of all things: I am He. Depart from thy father Terah and go out of his house, lest thou be consumed in his wickedness." And I went out; and it came to pass, as I came to the door of the house, that there fell a noise of a great thundering, and the fire fell and burned up my father Terah and his house and all that was therein.

This is the story of the beginning of the life of Abraham; and that which is told about the end of his life is as follows:

Abraham had lived out the measure of his days. He was now a hundred and seventy-five years old, and all the days of his life he had lived in kindness and meekness and uprightness: and especially was he hospitable and courteous to strangers. He dwelt by the cross-roads near the oak of Mamre, and entertained all the wayfarers who came that way, rich and poor, lame and sound, friends or strangers. But at last to him, as to all other men, there came the bitter cup of death, which none can put away. So when the time was come, the Most High called to him the archangel Michael and said to him, "Michael, prince of the host, go down to Abraham and speak to him concerning his death, that he may set his house in order: for his possessions are great. Announce to him therefore that he is to depart speedily out of the earthly life, and come to his Lord in peace and happiness."

Michael therefore went forth from the presence of the Lord and went down to Abraham at the oak of Mamre, and found him in the fields hard by, watching his husbandmen plowing with their oxen. And Abraham lifted up his eyes and saw Michael coming towards him in the dress and fashion of a soldier — for he was the captain of the Lord's host — very beautiful to look upon. And Abraham rose and went to meet him, as was his custom with all strangers; and when they had saluted one another, Abraham asked Michael whence he came; and Michael answered, "I come from the Great City, and my errand is to fetch a certain friend of the Great King, whom He is inviting to come to Him." Then said Abraham, "My lord, come with me to my house." And when Michael consented, Abraham called one of his men and bade him fetch two quiet horses that he and the stranger might ride home on them. But Michael refused, for he knew that no earthly horse could bear him; so he said, "Nay, but rather let us go on foot to your house."

And as they went up from the fields, they came to a cypress tree growing by the wayside; and as they passed by it there came from it a human voice, which said, "Holy is the Lord who calleth to Himself them that love Him." Now this happened by the commandment of God, to be a sign to Abraham, and he marveled; but when he looked at his companion and saw that he seemed to take no notice of it, he said nothing, thinking that only he had heard the voice. Soon after they came to the house, and Isaac and Sarah came to greet them, and they sat down in the courtyard of the house. But Isaac said to his mother Sarah, "Mother, I am sure that the man who is sitting with my father is not of the race of men that live on the earth." Just then Abraham called to Isaac, "Isaac, my son, draw water from the well, and bring it to me in a basin, that we may wash the stranger's feet, for he has come a long journey." So Isaac ran and fetched the water to his father; and Abraham said to him secretly, "My child, something says to me that this will be the last time that I shall wash the feet of any stranger coming to this house." And Isaac was greatly distressed and said, "What mean you, father, by these words?" Abraham said nothing, but stooped down and began to wash the feet of Michael; and Isaac wept. Abraham too shed tears, and Michael seeing it, was moved with pity, and wept also; and his tears fell into the basin of water and became precious pearls. When Abraham saw that, he marveled; but he gathered up the pearls secretly and said nothing.

After that he told Isaac to go and prepare the banqueting-room, spread two couches, light the lamps, burn sweet odors, and fetch fragrant herbs and flowers from the garden. "For," said he, "this man who is come to us is worthy of all the honor we can do him." So Isaac went to make ready the room, and Sarah also set about preparing a feast. Then, while they were all busying themselves with preparation, the sun began to set, and the hour came at which all the angels appear before God and worship Him; and Michael also flew up into the heavens in the twinkling of an eye, and stood before the Lord. And when all the angels had done their worship and gone forth again, Michael remained and said to the Lord, "Lord, I cannot speak to Abraham about his death; for I have never seen his like upon the earth, kind, courteous, hospitable, fearing God, and keeping himself pure from all evil. I cannot grieve his heart by telling him that he is to die." And the Lord said, "Go down again to my friend Abraham, and whatsoever he would have thee do, do it; and I will put the thought of his death into the mind of his son Isaac in a dream. Then Isaac shall tell the dream, and thou shalt interpret it, and so Abraham shall be certified of his death."

So Michael returned to Abraham's house, and sat at meat with him, and Isaac waited on them; and after supper, Abraham offered up prayer as he was wont, and the archangel prayed with him, and they went to their beds. Isaac also asked his father if he might sleep with them, for he desired exceedingly to be near the wonderful stranger and to hear his words; but Abraham said, "Nay, my son, lest we be burdensome to the stranger." Therefore Isaac bowed down and received his father's blessing, and went to his own chamber.

And about the third hour of the night Isaac dreamed a dream, and it frightened him, so that he leapt out of bed and ran hastily to the room where Abraham and Michael were sleeping, and beat upon the door and said, "Father, open to me quickly! let me kiss you once again before they take you away from me." Then Abraham opened the door, and Isaac ran in and hung upon his neck, weeping loudly. And Sarah was awakened by the noise of the weeping, and came quickly to them; and she also wept and said, "What is the matter? Has our brother who is come to us brought you evil tidings of Lot, your nephew?" But Michael said, "No, lady, it is not so; but, as I think, your son Isaac has dreamed a dream which has troubled him, so he came to us weeping, and we were moved at the sight of his tears, and wept with him."

Now Sarah, when she heard the sound of the voice of Michael, became sure in her own mind that it was an angel of God who was speaking. She beckoned therefore to Abraham to come to her at the door of the house, and took him aside and said to him, "Do you know who this man is?" and he said, "No." "Do you remember," said she, "the three men who came to us once at the oak of Mamre; and how you killed a calf and prepared a feast for them; and how when the calf was eaten, it suddenly became whole again and sprang up and ran and suckled its mother? I am sure that this is one of those three men." Abraham answered, "Sarah, you have hit the truth; praised be God for His wonders. Now I tell you that last night when I was washing the feet of this man, I said to myself, 'Surely these are the feet that I washed long ago under the oak tree?' And furthermore, he shed tears, and they fell into the water and became these pearls." And he drew the pearls out of his bosom and showed them to her, and she bowed her head and praised God and said, "Be sure, Abraham, that he is come to reveal some matter to us, whether for evil or for good."

Then Abraham left Sarah and went in and said to Isaac, "Come here, my child, and tell me what you saw, and what caused you to come to us in such haste?" And Isaac said, "It was this, father. I saw in a dream this night the sun and the moon upon my head, and the rays of the sun were all about me and enlightened me, and I rejoiced in them; then I saw the heavens opening, and a shining man, brighter than seven suns, came down; and he approached me and took the sun from off my head and carried it up into heaven; and again after a little while, as I was sorrowing over it, he came and took the moon from me. Then I was greatly distressed, and I besought him, saying, 'Nay, my lord, do not take all my glory from me; have pity upon me; if thou must needs take the sun, yet leave me the moon.' But he said, 'Suffer them to be taken up to the King above, for He desires them to be with Him.' So he took them away, saying, 'They are removed from toil unto rest, and from darkness unto light.' But their glory he left upon me. Then I awoke." And Isaac ceased speaking.

Then Michael said, "Hear me, righteous Abraham. The sun which Isaac saw is you, his father; the moon likewise is Sarah, his mother; and the shining one who came down out of heaven and took them away is myself. And now be it known to you that the time is come for you to leave this earthly life and go to God." But Abraham said, "Why, here is a marvel indeed! And are you the one appointed to take my soul from me?" He answered, "I am Michael, the captain of the host of God, and I am sent to speak to you concerning your death." Then said Abraham, "I know that you are an angel of God, and that you are sent to take away my soul. But I shall not follow you!"

When Michael heard that word he vanished away from them and went up to the heavens and stood before the Lord, and told Him what Abraham had said; and the Lord answered, "Return to Abraham My friend and speak yet again to him, Thus saith the Lord: 'I brought thee out of thy father's house into the land of promise: I have blessed thee and increased thee more than the sands of the seashore and more than the stars of heaven. Why dost thou resist My decree? Knowest thou not that Adam and Eve died, and all their offspring; none of the forefathers escaped death; they are all of them gone unto the place of spirits, all of them have been gathered by the sickle of death. And I have not suffered the angel of death to approach thee: I have not permitted any evil disease to come upon thee, but instead I have sent mine own prince Michael to speak peaceably unto thee, that thou mayest set thine house in order and bless thy son Isaac and depart in peace; and now thou sayest, "I will in nowise follow him." Knowest thou not that if I send Death unto thee, thou must needs come whether thou wilt or no?'" So Michael returned to Abraham, and found him weeping, and told him all these words; and Abraham besought him, saying, "Speak yet once again to my Lord and say to Him, 'Thus saith Abraham Thy servant: Lord, Thou hast been gracious to me all my life long, and now, behold, I do not resist Thy word, for I know that I am a mortal man; but this one thing I ask of Thee, that while I am yet in my body Thou wouldst suffer me to see Thy world and all the creatures that Thou hast made. Then shall I depart out of this life without any trouble of mind.'" And Michael returned and spake all these words before the Lord, and the Lord said, "Take a cloud of light and angels that have power over the chariots, and bear Abraham in the chariot of the cherubim into the air of heaven and let him see all the world before he dies."

And it was done; and Michael showed Abraham all the regions of the world. He saw men plowing and carting, keeping flocks, dancing, sporting, and playing the harp, wrestling, going to law, weeping, dying, and being carried out to burial: even all the things that are done in the earth, both good and evil. And in one place they saw men with swords in their hands, and Abraham asked Michael, "Who are these?" And Michael said, "These are thieves who are going out to steal and to kill and to destroy." Then Abraham said, "O that God would hear me and send evil beasts out of the forest to devour them!" And in that moment wild beasts rushed out upon them and tore them to pieces. Then in another place he saw men and women feasting and drinking before their idols, and he said, "O that the earth might open and swallow them up!" And immediately it happened as he had said. And in yet another place he saw me breaking through the wall of a house to enter it and rob it; and he prayed again, and fire fell from heaven and burned them up. Then there came a voice which said, "Michael, prince of My host, turn the chariot and bring Abraham back, lest, if he sees anymore of the sinners upon earth, he destroy the whole race of men. For he is a righteous man, and has no compassion upon sinners. But I created the world, and I would not have any perish. Bring Abraham therefore to the entering in of the gate of heaven, that he may see the judgment and the recompensing of men, and may have pity upon the souls whom he has blotted out."

Michael therefore turned the chariot and brought Abraham across the great river of Ocean to the entering in of the gate of heaven, and showed him the judgments. And Abraham saw the narrow gate of life and the broad gate of destruction, and between the gates he saw our father Adam sitting upon a throne, and clad in a glorious robe of many colors; and he saw how Adam lamented when the souls went in through the broad gate, and how he rejoiced when they attained to the narrow gate, and how his weeping exceeded his rejoicing. Moreover, Michael showed him how the souls of men are examined concerning their works and how their acts are re-corded and weighed. But when he saw how hard it is to enter in at the strait gate, it repented him that he had prayed for the punishment of the sinners, and he said to Michael, "O prince of the host, let us entreat the Lord that He would have mercy upon the souls of the men whom I cursed in my anger; for now I know that I sinned before God when I prayed against them." Then they both prayed earnestly to God; and after a long time there came a voice saying, "Abraham, I have heard thy prayer, and I have given back life to the men whom thou didst destroy."

Moreover, the voice bade Michael take Abraham back to his house. And when he was come thither, he went up to the great chamber, and sat upon the couch; and Sarah and Isaac came and fell on his neck, and all his servants gathered about him, rejoicing at his return. And Michael said, "Hearken, Abraham: here is Sarah your wife and Isaac your son, and here are all your manservants and maidservants about you. Now therefore set in order your house and bless them, and make ready to depart with me, for your hour is come." Abraham answered, "Did the Lord command you to say this, or do you say it of yourself?" Michael said, "The Lord commanded me, and I give the message to you." Yet for all that Abraham answered, "I will not follow you." So Michael went forth and stood before the Most High again and told him the words of Abraham; and he said besides, "I cannot lay hands upon him, for there is not his like upon the earth, no, not even the righteous Job. Tell me therefore, Lord, what I must do."

And God said, "Call Death, and bid him come hither." Michael went and found Death, and said to him, "Come, for the Lord of all things, the Immortal King, calleth for thee." And Death trembled and feared exceedingly when he heard that; but he followed Michael and came and stood before the Lord, quivering and shaking with fear, awaiting the commands of his Master. And God said to him, "Hide thy hideous appearance, cover up thy corruption, put away from thee all thy terror, and put on a glorious and beautiful aspect, and go down to Abraham My friend and take him and bring him to Me: only see that thou make him not afraid, but bring him peaceably, for he is My friend." So Death went forth from the presence of God, and made himself like an angel of light, beautiful to look upon, and departed to seek Abraham. Now Abraham had come down from his chamber and was sitting under the trees of Mamre, leaning his head upon his hand, expecting the return of Michael the archangel. And suddenly he was aware of a sweet perfume, and of a light shining near him; and he turned round and saw Death coming towards him in a form of great glory and beauty, and rose to meet him, supposing him to be an angel of God. And they greeted one another, and Abraham said, "Whence come you to me, and who are you?" Death answered, "Abraham, I tell you the truth: I am the bitter cup of death." Abraham said, "Rather you are the beauty of the world; a fairer than you I have never seen, and how say you, 'I am the bitter cup of death'?" He answered, "I have told you the truth; the name by which God named me is that which I have spoken." Abraham said, "And why have you come to this place?" Death answered, "I am come to take your soul, O righteous one." Abraham said, "I hear what you say, but I shall not come with you." But Death was silent and answered him not a word.

Then Abraham rose up and went towards his house: and Death followed him. And he went up into his chamber: and Death went with him; and he laid himself on his bed: and Death came and sat by his feet. And Abraham said, "Go, depart from me: I wish to rest here on my couch." Death answered, "I shall not depart till I have taken thy soul from thy body." Abraham said, "I adjure thee by the living God: art thou in very truth Death?" He said, "I am." Then said Abraham, "Comest thou to all men in such a beautiful shape as this?" He said, "Nay, my lord Abraham; it is thy righteousness and thy good deeds which make as it were a crown of glory upon my head; it is only to such as thou art that I come thus peaceably, but to sinners I show myself much otherwise." "Show me then," said Abraham, "in what form thou comest to them: let me see all thy fierceness and bitterness." "No," said Death, "for thou couldst not bear to look upon it." "Verily, I am able to bear it," he said, "for the strength of the God of heaven is with me."

Then Death let fall from him all his beauty, and Abraham saw him as he was. And where there had been a shining angel, he saw a cloud of darkness, and in it the shapes of horrible wild beasts and all unclean creatures; and he saw the heads of fiery dragons, and flames of consuming fire darting out; and he seemed to see a dreadful precipice before him, and then a rushing river, and flashes of lightning, and crackling of thunder, and thereafter a tempestuous raging sea; and again weapons brandished, and venomous basilisks and serpents, and bowls of poison; and there came a horrible odor, so that all the servants of Abraham that were in the chamber fainted and died, and Abraham himself swooned and his senses left him.

When he came to himself, Death had hidden his terrible aspect and put on his beautiful form again. And Abraham saw his servants lying dead, and said to Death, "How is it that thou hast slain these?" And Death said, "They died at the sight of my countenance, and in truth it is a marvel that thou also didst not die with them." "Yea," said Abraham, "now I know how it was that I came by this faintness of spirit that is upon me; but I pray thee, Death, inasmuch as these have been cut off before their time, let us entreat God that he would raise them up again." So Abraham and Death prayed together; and the spirit of life returned into the servants that had been killed, and they rose up again. After that Abraham conversed with Death.

Then Sarah and Isaac came in and talked with Abraham as he lay on his bed. And Abraham said to Death, "I beseech thee, depart from me for a little, for since I looked upon thee weakness is come upon me, and my breath labors and my heart is troubled." Then said Death, "Kiss my right hand and thy strength will return to thee, and thou wilt be filled with joy." So Abraham kissed the hand of Death, and the soul of Abraham clave to the hand of Death and left his body; and straightway Michael was there and a multitude of angels with him, and they accompanied the holy soul of Abraham and brought it into the heavens into the presence of the Most High, there to abide everlastingly in gladness and brightness in the place from which all sorrow and sighing are fled away.

The Story of Aseneth, Joseph's Wife

I

*T*here was once a great man named Potipherah, who was high priest of the city of On in Egypt; and he and his wife had no children. One day he went into the temple to offer sacrifice, as was his custom. He went alone, and when he entered the great courtyard of the temple, in the middle of which stood the altar, he was astonished to see a little child lying upon the altar. Without waiting to offer his sacrifice, he hurried back to his wife. "What is the matter," said she, "that you come back so hastily?" "I have seen a wonderful thing," he said; "the gods have given us a child. The gates of the temple were locked, so that no one could get into the court; yet there is a child there, lying on the altar!" "What say you?" said his wife; "what can be the meaning of it?" So they both hastened to the temple, and when Potipherah opened the door of the courtyard, they saw, partly at least, how the wonder had happened; for now there was an eagle perched upon the altar with its wings spread out over the child — it was a little girl, quite newly born — to protect it. They guessed that it was the eagle that had brought the child, but, of course, they could not tell whose it was. It was wrapped in swaddling-clothes, and these Potipherah's wife kept carefully by her; for she thought the time might come when they might be recognized by the parents of the little child; and indeed, years afterwards, this proved to be the case.

In the meantime Potipherah and his wife kept the child and brought her up, and treated her as their daughter; and they called her Aseneth.

She grew up to be very beautiful; she was quite unlike an Egyptian girl, and might have been taken for a Hebrew maiden: tall as Sarah and lovely as Rebekah or Rachel; so beautiful, in fact, that all the sons of the princes and nobles of Egypt were in love with her, and even the son of King Pharaoh himself said to his father, "Give me Aseneth, the daughter of Potipherah, to wife." But Pharaoh said, "Nay, my son, she is not of your rank; you must marry a queen; remember, the daughter of the King of Moab is affianced to you."

But besides being very beautiful, Aseneth was exceedingly proud. There was not a man of all the young nobles whom she would hear of, much less look at. Indeed, hardly any man in Egypt except her own father had ever seen her face; for she lived apart with the maidens who waited on her, in a lofty tower which her father had built specially for her. It was really a noble palace, with ten great rooms, one over the other. The first room was paved with porphyry and lined with slabs of colored marbles, and the roof was of gold: and it was a kind of chapel for Aseneth. It had golden and silver images of all the gods of Egypt, and Aseneth worshipped them and burned incense to them every day. The second chamber was Aseneth's own. In it were all her jewels and rich robes and fine linen. In the third were stored the provisions of the house and every delicious fruit or sweetmeat that could be got from any part of the world. The other seven chambers belonged to the seven maidens who lived with Aseneth and tended her. They were all of one age, and as fair as the stars of heaven, and Aseneth loved them dearly.

But to come back to Aseneth's own chamber, which was the most splendid of all. It had three windows, one looking out upon the garden of the tower towards the east, and another towards the south, and the third towards the high-road. Opposite the eastern window stood a golden bed, with a coverlet woven of gold and purple and fine linen.

And no one but Aseneth herself had ever even sat upon that bed, so magnificent and so sacred was it.

Besides all this, the tower had all around it a garden with a high wall of squared blocks of stone. The gates (there were four of them) were of iron, and each was guarded by eighteen stalwart men in armor. The garden itself was full of shady trees, bearing splendid fruit, and there was a springing fountain at one side of it, whose water ran first into a marble trough, and then out of that into a stream which watered all the garden and kept it fresh and green.

Here Aseneth lived until she was eighteen years old, beautiful and proud and caring for no one except her father and mother and her seven maidens. Now the year in which she became eighteen was the first of the seven years of plenty, of which King Pharaoh had dreamt in the dream of the seven cows and the seven ears of corn, which is written in the Bible. And Joseph was now traveling over all the land of Egypt to gather together corn to store up against the seven years of famine which were to follow the seven of plenty. And upon a certain day in harvest-time, Potipherah and his

wife, who had been away at an estate which they possessed in the country, returned to the city of On; and
no sooner had they done so than they received a
message from Joseph, saying, "Let me come and rest at
your house during the heat of the day." Whereupon
Potipherah was greatly rejoiced, and thanked the gods
for the honor which Joseph did him by visiting him,
and ordered a great banquet to be prepared.

Just at this time, Aseneth, who had heard that her
father and mother were returned, came to meet them.
She had put on her most beautiful robe, of linen woven
with gold, and a golden girdle, and necklace and brace-
lets of precious stones upon which were engraved the
names of the gods of Egypt. And she had a golden
diadem on her head, and over it a delicate veil. She
hastened to meet her father and mother, and they
rejoiced at her wonderful beauty, and made her sit by
them, and showed her the gifts they had brought to
her from the country — grapes and figs, pomegranates
and fresh dates, and young doves and quails for her to
tame, to her great delight. Then her father said to her,
"My child, sit here with us: I want to speak to you."
So she sat down between her father and mother, and
her father took her hand and kissed her, and said, "My
darling child, do you know that Joseph, the lord of all
this land, the man who is going to save the country
from the famine that is coming the man whom Pharaoh trusts and honors above all others, is coming to
this house today? What would you say if I were to offer
to give you in marriage to him, to live happily with
him for the rest of your life?"

Then Aseneth was very angry; she blushed as red as
fire, and darted an ugly glance at her father sideways,
and said, "How can you talk to me so, father? Would
you give me to a creature like that, the son of a
Ganaanitish laborer, who has been in prison — yes, and

sold as a slave — and only got out of prison because he contrived to explain a dream of Pharaoh's, for all the world like the old women? Certainly not! If I marry anyone it will be Pharaoh's eldest son." So Potipherah, disappointed as he was, said no more; and Aseneth hurried away to her own chamber. But she looked out of the window.

As she went out, there ran in a young man, one of Potipherah's servants, and said, "My lord, Joseph is just stopping before our gates." So Potipherah and his wife and all their retinue rose and went forth to meet Joseph; and the gates of the court towards the east were thrown open, and the chariot drove in, drawn by four milk-white horses with harness of gold; and in the chariot stood Joseph, clad in a tunic of white linen and a blood-red mantle shot with gold. On his head was a crown with twelve great gems, and above each gem was a ray of gold; in his hand was an olive branch with leaves and fruit. But fairer than all his equipment was his face, for he was more beautiful than any of the sons of men. And just as all the young nobles of Egypt were mad about Aseneth, so all the ladies of Egypt were in love with Joseph; but he had not a word to say to any of them, for they were all worshippers of idols, and Joseph worshipped the true God — the God of Abraham, Isaac, and Jacob.

So the chariot entered the courtyard of Poti-pherah's palace, and the gates were shut. Now Aseneth stood at her window, and when she saw Joseph and the beauty of his countenance, she was smitten to the heart, her knees trembled, and she almost swooned. A great fear came upon her, and she heaved a deep sigh and said, "Alas, alas, what have I said? what have I done? Pity me, O God of Joseph, for it was in ignorance that I spoke against him. Did I not call him a Canaanitish laborer's son? and lo, now he has come into our house like the sun out of heaven. Fool that I was to rail against him as I did! If only my father would give me to him as his slave and drudge, I would serve him till I dropped dead at his feet."

Meanwhile Joseph, who had caught sight of Aseneth standing at her window, had come into the house, and they had washed his feet and set a table for him by himself (for Joseph would not eat with the Egyptians). And he said to Potipherah, "Who was the woman whom I saw looking out of the window when I came in? Some stranger? If so, she must leave this house." "Nay, my lord," said Potipherah, "she is our daughter." And he went on to tell how Aseneth disliked the company of men, and indeed had hardly seen a strange man before that day; and Joseph was glad to hear that she hated strange men, and said, "If she be your daughter, I will love her from this day forth as a sister."

Accordingly, Aseneth's mother went and fetched Aseneth, and she greeted Joseph, and he her. Then said Potipherah, "Come near, my child, and kiss your brother." But when she drew near, Joseph put out his hand and thrust her away, and spoke thus: "It is not right for one who worships the living God, and eats the bread of life and drinks the cup of immortality, to kiss one that praises with her lips dead idols, and eats the bread of death from their tables and drinks the cup of deceit." At these harsh words Aseneth was bitterly grieved: she shrank back and looked piteously at Joseph, and her eyes filled with tears; and when he saw how hurt she was, Joseph, who was full of kindness raised his hand over her head and blessed her, praying that God, who gives life to all and brings us out of darkness into light, might give life and light to her soul, and number her among His chosen people, and bring her into the everlasting rest which He has promised to them. So Aseneth went back to her chamber, full of mingled joy and sorrow; and she cast herself down on her bed and wept. And that same evening Joseph left the house of Potipherah and set forth on his journey again. "But," said he, "I will come back to you in eight days' time." Potipherah also and his wife and their servants went back to their country house; and Aseneth and her seven maidens were left alone. And the sun went down and all was quiet.

II

*W*hen everyone else in the tower was asleep, Aseneth, who had remained weeping on her bed, rose up stealthily and crept downstairs to the gate of the tower, where the woman who kept the door was asleep with her children; and as quietly as she could she unhooked the heavy leather curtain that hung in the doorway, and spreading it out on the floor, heaped up upon it all the cinders and ashes out of the hearth, folded the corners together, dragged it upstairs and threw it down on the floor. Then she barred the door of her room securely, and burst into bitter weeping. It so happened that the maiden whom Aseneth loved the best of all her seven companions was awake, and heard the sounds of crying. She was alarmed, and flew to wake up the other attendants, and all of them came to the door of Aseneth's chamber, which was locked and barred. They called to her, "What is the matter, dear mistress? Open to us and let us come in and comfort you." But Aseneth answered from within, "It is nothing but a violent headache. I am in bed, and too tired and ill to get up and open the door. Go back all of you to your beds. I shall be well tomorrow." So they dispersed to their rooms.

And when they were safely gone, Aseneth got up and opened the door of the room in which she kept her dresses and jewels, taking care to make no noise; and from among all her robes she chose out a black one which she had worn, years before, when the only son of Potipherah had died. And she cast off her royal robe and her diadem and veil and girdle, and put on the black robe and girded it with a rope. Next she went to the shrine wherein stood all the golden and silver images of her gods, and took them and threw them out of the window for the wayfarers to pick up; and she took the supper that had been laid out for her of all manner of delicate meats, and threw that into the highway for the dogs to eat. And she emptied the ashes out of the leather curtain upon the floor; she let down her hair and cast some of the ashes upon her head; she smote her breast and wept; and thus she sat in silence and misery till seven days and nights were accomplished.

And on the morning of the eighth day, when it was just dawning, and the birds had begun to twitter in the trees of the garden, and the dogs to bark at the passers-by, Aseneth raised herself a little from her crouching posture among the ashes and turned herself to the window that looked towards the east. She was faint and ill and weary from her long fasting and watching; her tongue was dry as horn, her eyes were glazed, and her fair face was haggard. She bent her head down and clasped her hands together, and crouched down again among the ashes, and said to herself, "It is all over. I have no one to turn to now. My father and mother will cast me off, for I have dishonored their gods; they will say, 'Aseneth is no daughter of ours.' My kindred will hate me, and all the youths whom I have despised and rejected will rejoice at my humiliation; and Joseph will have nothing to say to me because I am a foul worshipper of idols. Yet," she went on to say, "I have heard that the God of the Hebrews is a merciful God, long-suffering and compassionate, not hard upon those that have sinned ignorantly, if they are sorry for what they have done. Why should I not turn to Him? Who knows if He will not have pity upon my loneliness and protect me? For they say He is the Father of the fatherless, and cares for those who are in trouble." So she rose and knelt upon her knees, with her face turned towards the east, and looked up into heaven and prayed. "Save me," she said, "from those who are pursuing me, before I am caught by them; as a little child when it is frightened runs to its father, and the father stretches out his arms and catches it to his breast, so I flee to Thee. I know that Satan, the Old Lion, is hunting me; for he is the father of the gods of Egypt, and I have insulted them and destroyed their images. I have no hope but in Thee. See, I have cast off all my beautiful robes and ornaments; I sit here in sackcloth and ashes; I have fasted and wept these seven days, because I know that I have done wrong in worshipping dumb idols, and in speaking scornfully against Joseph. But, Lord, I did it in ignorance; save me, and above all watch over Joseph, whom I love more than my own life. Keep him, Lord, in safety, and let me be his handmaid and his slave, if Thou wilt, so that I may minister to him all the days I have to live."

Much more did Aseneth say in her prayer, but it is not written down here. When she had ended, the morning star was just coming up in the east, and Aseneth rejoiced when she saw it and said, "Can it be that God has heard my prayer, and that this star is the

herald of the light of the great day?" Then, in that part
of the sky where the star was shining, there opened a
little cleft in the heavens, and a bright light shone out
of it: so dazzling that she fell on her face upon the
ashes. And in the next instant there stood over her a
man who was all flashing with light; and he called to
her, "Aseneth, rise up." "Who can this be who calls
me?" she said; "my door is barred and the tower is high.
No one can have come into my chamber." So she did
not look up; but the man called to her again, "Aseneth,
Aseneth!" And at last she answered, "Here am I, lord:
tell me, who art thou?" He answered, "I am the Prince
of all the army of heaven; rise up and stand on your
feet, and hear my words." Then for the first time she
looked at him, and saw that he was in all things like
Joseph, with royal robe, and crown and scepter; but his
face, and hair, and hands and feet were bright like the
sun, and his eyes pierced like lightning; and again she
was afraid, and fell on her face. But he said, "Do not
be afraid; hear what I am come to say to you." Thereupon she rose and stood up, weak as she was; and he
bade her go into her inner chamber and put off her
black robe, and the sackcloth and ashes, and bathe
herself in clear water, and array herself in the noblest
of her robes, and come back to him.

Now when this was done, and she had returned to
him, fresh and beautiful as formerly, he spoke kindly
to her, and blessed her and said, "God has heard your
prayer: He has looked upon your sorrow and tears, and
has forgiven your sin. Be of good cheer, for your name
is written in the Book of Life, and shall no more be
blotted out. From this day forth you shall eat the bread
of life and drink the cup of immortality, and be
anointed with the oil of joy. And a new name shall be
given you, even the name of the City of Refuge; for as
you have come to God for refuge, many shall in like

manner come to Him through your example by repentance. And now, behold, this day I shall go to Joseph,
and tell him that which has befallen you, and he shall
come to you this very day and make you his bride.
Make ready therefore and array yourself in the bridal
robe that is laid up in your chamber, and put upon
you all your elect ornaments, and prepare yourself to
meet him."

When Aseneth heard this joyful news, she fell on her
face at the feet of the messenger and gave thanks to
God; and, said she, "My lord, stay yet a little while, I
pray you, and sit upon this couch, and I will set a table
before you, and bread, and you shall eat; and I will
bring you wine old and fragrant, and you shall drink,
and so go on your way." For she did not know that it
was an angel who had come to her. And he said, "I will
do so: hasten therefore and make ready."

So first she set before him a table; and as she was
going to fetch the bread he said to her, "Bring a
honeycomb also." But at this she stopped, and was
troubled in her mind, for she knew that there was no
honeycomb in her store-room. "Why do you stop?"
said the angel. "Sir," she answered, "let me send a boy
to the farm which is near by, and he shall fetch you a
honeycomb in a moment." "No," said he, "you need
only go into your store-room, and you will find one
upon the table; bring that to me." "Sir," she answered,
"I know that there is none there." But he said, "Go and
you will find it." She went therefore and found the
honeycomb, as he had said; it was large, and as white
as snow, and full of honey, and the smell of it was as
the breath of life. She wondered greatly, but she would
not delay, and she brought it out and put it on the
table before the angel. Then he called her to him, and
as she moved towards him he stretched out his right
hand over her head, and again she was afraid, for she

saw sparks and flashes of fire coming from it, as if it were of heated iron; so that she gazed upon him earnestly in astonishment. But he smiled and said, "You are blessed, Aseneth, for you have seen some of the secret things of God; it is of this honeycomb that the angels eat in Paradise, and the bees of Paradise have made it of the dew of the roses of life in the garden of God; and whosoever tastes it shall not die forever." Then he put forth his right hand and took a piece of the honeycomb, and tasted it, and gave a portion to Aseneth, and she ate it; and he said, "Now you have received the food of life, and your youth shall know no old age, and your beauty shall never fade." And again he stretched forth his right hand and drew his finger across the honeycomb from the east side of it to the west, and from the north side to the south, and where his finger touched it there was left a track of the color of blood. And immediately there came out of the honeycomb a multitude of bees. They were white like snow, and their wings were purple and scarlet, and they swarmed about Aseneth and made honey upon her lips. Among them there were some that made as though they would have stung her, but these the angel rebuked, and they fell to the ground dead. But after a while the angel said to the bees, "Go to your place," and at that they rose up in a swarm and flew out of the window and up into the sky. Then he touched with his rod the dead bees upon the floor, and said to them, "Go ye also to your place," and they came to life and flew out of the window, and settled upon the trees in the garden of Aseneth. And for the third time he stretched out his hand and touched the honeycomb upon the table, and straightway there burst forth a flame, and consumed the honeycomb — but upon the table it left no mark — and the sweet smell of the burning filled all the chamber.

Then said Aseneth, "Sir, I have seven companions, maidens who have been brought up with me, and I love them as sisters: may I not call them, and you shall bless them as you have blessed me?" So she called them in, and made them stand before the angel, and he blessed them; and thereafter he said to Aseneth, "Take away the table." And as she turned aside to lift it, he was gone. But through the window she saw in the sky a chariot and four horses shining like fire, going into the heavens towards the east, and the angel standing in the chariot. Then she said, "Ah, foolish that I am! I knew not that it was an angel out of heaven that came into my chamber, and now, behold, he is going back into heaven to his own place. Pardon me, my lord, and spare thy handmaid, for it was in ignorance that I spoke so boldly before thee!"

While she was still wondering, there came in a messenger and said, "Joseph, the mighty one of God, is on his way hither." And immediately Aseneth sent for the steward of the palace and bade him prepare a great banquet, and make all things ready; but she herself, remembering the words of the angel, went into her inner chamber and adorned herself as a bride, in shining robes, and upon her head she put a crown of gold which had in the midst, over her forehead, a great jacinth stone and six other precious stones round it; and she covered her head with a veil of wonderful beauty. Then she called to one of her maidens, who brought her a basin of pure water, and when she saw the reflection of her face in the water she was astonished at the beauty and freshness and brightness of it. Just then the steward of the palace came in to say that all was ready, and he too was struck with amazement at the sight of her, and said, "Lady, what is the cause of this wonderful beauty? Can it be that the God of heaven has chosen you to be the bride of Joseph,

His elect?" And while he was yet speaking, the sound of Joseph's chariot-wheels was heard without.

Then Aseneth hastened and went down to meet Joseph, and her seven maidens followed her, and they all stood in the porch of the palace. And when Joseph saw Aseneth he also marveled, and said, "Who art thou, maiden?" And she answered, "Thy handmaid Aseneth; and I have cast away all my idols and they are gone." And she went on and told him of the coming of the angel to her. And he rejoiced. Then they came near and embraced one another, and she led him into her father's house and made him sit on her father's throne; and Joseph said, "Let one of the maidens come and wash my feet." But Aseneth said, "No; from henceforth I am your handmaid: your hands are my hands, your feet are my feet, and your soul is my soul: none other shall wash your feet but I." So she compelled him, and washed his feet. And after that he kissed her again, and made her sit down beside him, on his right hand.

And as they were talking together, Potipherah and his wife and their household entered the palace, having returned from the country; and they were amazed, and rejoiced at the sight of Joseph and Aseneth. And when they learnt all that had happened, they rejoiced yet more; and Potipherah said, "Tomorrow I will call together all my kinsfolk and prepare your marriage feast." But Joseph said, "Nay, but I will first go to Pharaoh and speak to him concerning Aseneth, that I may take her to wife; for he is to me as a father."

So on the next day Joseph departed to see Pharaoh, and forthwith Pharaoh sent for Potipherah and his wife and Aseneth; and in their presence he blessed Aseneth, and joined her hand with the hand of Joseph, and crowned them with golden crowns, and made a great feast for them lasting seven days; and all the land of Egypt rejoiced. So Joseph and Aseneth were married;

and after that two sons were born to them, even Ephraim and Manasseh, in the house of Joseph.

III

Now when the seven years of plenty were over, the years of famine began, and Jacob and his sons came to dwell in Egypt in the land of Goshen, as it is told in the Bible. Then Aseneth said to Joseph, "Let me go and see your father and greet him." So Joseph brought her to Jacob, and his brethren met him and did him obeisance at the door of the house, and they entered in. And when they saw Jacob, who was sitting upon his bed, Aseneth was struck with amazement at the sight of him, for he was noble to look upon. His head was white as snow, his beard was long, flowing over his bosom, his eyes were bright and flashing, and his muscles and limbs were those of a giant. And Aseneth fell on her face before him; and Israel said, "Is this thy wife, my son Joseph? Blessed shall she be of the Most High God." Then he called her to him, and she fell on his breast and he kissed her, and they rejoiced together. After that he inquired of her concerning her parents; and Aseneth told him how an eagle had brought her and laid her upon the altar of the temple of On; and she showed him the swaddling-clothes in which she had been wrapped. And Jacob knew that they belonged to his own daughter Dinah; and thus it was made known to him that Aseneth was of his own race, and he was the more glad.

And when they departed from him, Simeon and Levi accompanied them with the other sons of Leah and Rachel; but the sons of Bilhah and Zilpah would not go with them, for they hated Joseph. And of all Joseph's brethren, Aseneth loved Levi the most, for he was a prophet and a seer, and could read the signs of the stars of heaven.

Now it happened that as they were on their way to visit Jacob, the eldest son of Pharaoh was on the city wall, and he saw Aseneth and loved her immediately, and could think of nothing but how he might make away with Joseph and take Aseneth for his own wife. And after a few days he sent secretly to Simeon and Levi, and said to them, "I know that you are mighty men, and that with your two swords alone you defeated the men of Shechem and overthrew their city. I have sent for you because I wish to make you my friends, and, if you will do what I ask you, I will give you riches and lands and houses — in a word, all that you can desire. Now what I would have you do is this. You must know that I have been bitterly wronged by your brother Joseph: he has married Aseneth, who was betrothed to me long ago. Join with me therefore and help me to kill him, and I will take Aseneth to wife, and you shall be my brothers. If you refuse, I will slay you." And with these words he drew his sword and flourished it at them. At this Simeon, who was a man of hot temper, was enraged, and would have drawn his own sword and cut down the prince; but Levi, who could read his thoughts, trod upon his foot and made signs to him to be quiet, and whispered, "Why be angry with this fellow? We are God-fearing men, and must not render evil for evil." Then Levi said calmly and mildly to Pharaoh's son, "Why does my lord speak thus to his servants? We can do no such wickedness against our brother and against our God. Let us hear no more such evil words; but, if you will not be persuaded, know that our swords will be drawn against you." With that both the brothers drew their swords, and when the son of Pharaoh saw them he crouched upon the ground in terror, for they flashed like flames of fire and dazzled his eyes. But Levi said, "Get up and do not be frightened: only take care that you say nothing more of this kind against our brother Joseph." And they went forth from his presence.

But he could not restrain himself, for he was half-mad with anger and fear and with love of Aseneth. And after some days his servants said to him, "Do you know that the sons of Bilhah and Zilpah are at enmity with Joseph and Aseneth? They will do all that you ask of them." So he sent for them, for Dan and Gad and Naphtali and Asher, and they came to him in the first hour of the night; and after he had greeted them he sent away his servants, and said to the brethren, "Listen to me. Life and death are before you; choose which you will have: will you die like women or fight like men? I overheard your brother Joseph saying to my father Pharaoh, 'Dan and Gad and Naphtali and Asher are no brethren of mine; they are the sons of my father's handmaids, and I am only waiting till my father dies to make an end of them and their families. It was they who sold me to the Ishmaelites, and I am going to repay it into their bosom.' And my father said, 'It is well spoken: you have leave to take any of my bodyguard and deal with them as you will.'" Then Dan and Gad and their brothers were sorely troubled, and they said, "O sir, help us, and we will be your servants forever." And he said, "I will. Hear me now: this night I will kill my father Pharaoh — for he is the helper of Joseph — and do you for your part slay Joseph. Then I will take Aseneth to wife, and you shall be my brethren and joint heirs with me in the kingdom." So they said, "We will do so, and thus it shall be: we heard Joseph say to Aseneth that she should go tomorrow into the vineyard, for it is the time of vintage. We therefore will go this night into the bed of the river and hide among the reeds; and do you take with you fifty archers upon horses, and go on before. Then will Aseneth come and fall into our ambush, and we will kill the men that are with her, and she will flee in her chariot and fall into your hands, and you shall do to her as seems good to you. As for Joseph, while he is mourning for Aseneth we will kill him; but first we will slay his children before his face." And Pharaoh's son rejoiced greatly, and sent them forth with a great body of mighty men, and they went and hid themselves in four companies among the reeds of the river on either side of the road.

Yet Naphtali and Asher murmured against their elder brothers Dan and Gad, saying, "To what purpose are you conspiring again? Did you not sell Joseph for a slave before, and, lo! he is become lord over all Egypt? Now therefore, if you imagine evil against him, he will call upon God, and fire will come down out of heaven and devour you, and the angels of God will fight against you." But their elder brothers were angry and said, "What then would you have? Are we to die like women? Not so!" And the counsel of Naphtali and Asher did not prevail with them.

In the same night the son of Pharaoh rose up and went to his father's chamber with intent to slay him, as he had promised; but when he came to the door the guards stopped him and said, "What is my lord's will?" He said, "I desire to see my father, for I am going away tomorrow to visit my vine-yard which I have newly planted." And they said, "Your father is ill and has not slept until now, and he gave us commandment that no man should come into his chamber, no, not if it were his firstborn son." So he went away in a rage, and took fifty archers with him on horses and went on before, as Dan and Gad had said.

Aseneth also arose early in the morning and said to Joseph, "Lo, I go to the vineyard as you appointed; but my soul is troubled greatly at being parted from you." But Joseph said, "Be of good cheer; the Lord is with you and will keep you as the apple of an eye. As for me, I go to distribute corn to the people of the land, that no man in Egypt may perish of hunger." So Aseneth went her way; and as she came to the place of the ambush by the river, the men that were in hiding rushed out upon her, and slew all the guard that were with her, even six hundred soldiers and fifty runners; and Aseneth fled away upon her chariot.

Now Levi, though he was afar off, saw in the spirit what was being done — for he was a seer — and told his brethren of the peril of Aseneth; and they girded every man his sword upon his thigh, and took up their shields and their spears and ran swiftly after Aseneth.

And as she fled on before, suddenly she saw the son of Pharaoh in the way, and the horsemen that were with him. Then was Aseneth in great fear, and she called upon the name of her God.

But Benjamin was in the chariot with her. Now he was a lad of nineteen years, beautiful exceedingly, and strong as a lion's whelp. And when he saw the men, he leapt down from the chariot and caught up a round stone out of the brook and threw it at the son of Pharaoh, and smote him on the left temple, so that he fell from his horse half-dead.

Then Benjamin leapt up upon a rock by the way-side, and called to the driver of the chariot, "Give me stones out of the river bed." And he gave them; and with fifty stones Benjamin slew the fifty archers that were with

Pharaoh's son; every stone smote a man on the temples.

Moreover, the sons of Leah, Reuben and Simeon, Levi and Judah, Issachar and Zebulun, pursued after the men that had laid wait for Aseneth, and fell upon them suddenly and cut them to pieces; but the sons of Bilhah and Zilpah fled before them, saying, "We are undone; and now, behold, the son of Pharaoh is dead, and all they that were with him. Let us at least slay Aseneth and Benjamin, and flee into the woods." So they pursued after Aseneth, and came upon her with their swords drawn and dripping with blood. And she was greatly afraid, and said, "Lord God, who didst save me from false gods and from the corruption of death, and didst say, 'Thy soul shall live forever,' save me now from the hands of these wicked men!" And God heard her prayer, and straightway the swords of the men fell out of their hands and crumbled into dust.

Then they were very sore afraid, saying, "The Lord fighteth against us." And they fell down on their faces and besought Aseneth, saying, "We have imagined evil against you, and the Lord hath brought it back upon us. But now have pity upon us, and save us from the wrath of our brethren." And she said, "Go then and hide yourselves in the reeds until I appease them and turn away their anger. Only the Lord be judge betwixt me and you." Then they ran and hid among the reeds; and their brethren the sons of Leah came running like harts to overtake them. And Aseneth lighted down from her chariot and fell on their necks weeping and rejoicing; and they said, "Where are our brothers the sons of the handmaids?" that they might kill them. But Aseneth said, "I beseech you, spare them, for the Lord saved me out of their hands and broke their swords, and, behold, there they lie, like wax melted before the fire. Let it suffice you that the Lord hath fought against them on our behalf, and spare them, for they are your brethren and the sons of your father Israel." Then said Simeon, "Why doth our sister say so? Nay, but we will hew them in pieces with our swords, for they have done evil against Joseph and against our father and against thee also this day." And Aseneth took hold upon Simeon's beard and kissed him, and said, "Do not, my brother, in anywise render evil for evil: the Lord shall judge between us; and now, see, they are fled afar off. Forgive them, therefore, and spare their lives." Then Levi came near and kissed her right hand; for he knew that his brethren were in hiding among the reeds, but he would not reveal it to the others lest they should fall upon them; and he loved Aseneth because she would save them alive.

Now the son of Pharaoh, who was fallen from his horse, began to recover himself, and sat up and spat blood out of his mouth, for the blood ran down from the wound on his temple into his mouth. And Benjamin saw it, and ran and drew the sword of the son of Pharaoh (for as yet Benjamin bare no sword upon his thigh), and would have slain him; but Levi hasted and caught his hand, saying, "It is not right for us that fear God to trample upon him that is fallen, or to afflict our enemy to death. Put back the sword into its place and help me, and we will tend his wound, and if he lives he shall be our friend." Then Levi helped up the son of Pharaoh from the ground, and washed the blood from his face and bound up his wound with a bandage, and put him upon his horse and took him to Pharaoh his father, and told him all that had happened. And Pharaoh rose up from his throne and blessed Levi. But on the third day after, the son of Pharaoh died of his wound.

And Pharaoh mourned sore for his firstborn son, insomuch that he fell sick and died, being a hundred and nine years old, and left his crown to Joseph; and Joseph reigned alone in Egypt forty and eight years, and thereafter gave the kingdom to the younger son of Pharaoh, who was a sucking child when his father died. And thenceforth Joseph was called the father of the king throughout all the land of Egypt.

Job

*T*his is the story of the life of Job, taken out of the book called The Testament of Job.

There came a day when Job felt that his end was near, and he called together his seven sons and his three daughters, and said to them:

Come near to me, my children, and I will tell you the story of my life, and all the dealings of the Lord with me. You must know, in the first place, that before He gave me a new name, I was called Jobab; and that I come of the family of Isaac — for I am one of the sons of Esau, Jacob's brother. Now, long ago, I used to dwell hard by the temple of an idol, and every day I saw people coming and bringing offerings, and burning sacrifices before it. But as time went on, I could not believe that this idol was indeed the God who made the heavens, and the earth, and the sea, and us men. I pondered much, therefore, upon this matter, saying, "How shall I come to know the truth of it?"

Thereafter, as I lay upon my bed, in the middle of the night, a bright light suddenly shone in my chamber, and I heard a voice calling me, "Jobab, Jobab!" (and I answered, "Here am I"). And the voice said, "Rise up, and I will tell thee that which I have to say. Verily, this idol to whom offerings are brought, and wine poured out in libations, is not a god, but is a work of the evil power whereby he deceives the sons of men." Then I bowed myself down and said, "Lord, who hast come to enlighten my soul, I beseech thee, give me leave to go and cleanse this place that is polluted by the enemy, so that offerings shall no more be made to him; but, indeed, who is there that can withstand me, seeing that I am ruler over this country?"

The voice answered me out of the light, "Thou canst indeed destroy that place; but I must forewarn thee of that which will ensue, according as I have in hand to tell thee from the Lord." And I answered, "All that He commandeth thy servant will I hear and do." And the voice said again, "If thou takest upon thee to destroy this abode of Satan's, he will rise up and fight against thee; he will bring upon thee many plagues; he will take away all thy gods; he will slay thy children. Only he will not be able to take thy life. And, if thou endurest to the end, thy name shall become famous among all generations forever; and I will restore thee to thy former estate, and recompense thee double, and thou shalt rise up again in the resurrection of the just. Be thou therefore like a fighter who giveth blows and endureth them, looking to win the crown of victory; and then shalt thou know that the Lord is righteous, and true, and mighty, giving strength to His chosen."

And I, my children, answered him, "I will verily endure even unto death, and will not draw back." Then the angel set a mark upon my forehead, and departed from me; and in the same night I arose and gathered to me fifty of my servants, and went and destroyed the temple of the idol, laying it even with the ground. Then I returned to my house, and commanded that the doors should be made fast.

Hearken now, my children, and wonder; for as soon as I had come into my house, and had commanded the doors to be shut, and had told the keepers of the doors to say to any that came that I was not at leisure to see them, Satan came, having put on the appearance of a beggar, and said to the maid that kept the door, "Tell Job that I desire to speak with him." She came to me, therefore, and I told her again, "Tell him that I have no leisure to see him."

So Satan departed, and took on him another form, and put a wallet on his shoulder, and returned and said to the maid, "Say to Job, 'Give me bread from thine own hand, that I may eat.'" Then I took a loaf that was burned black and gave it to the maid to give to him, saying, "Look to eat no more of my bread, for I am become a stranger to you." But the maid was ashamed to give him the burned bread, for she knew not who he was; she took, therefore, a good loaf of her own and gave it to him. But he was aware of what had happened, and said to her, "Go back, unfaithful servant, and fetch me the bread that was given to you to give to me!" And she wept and said, "You say well that I am an unfaithful servant, for I have not done that which I was commanded." Then she brought him the burned bread, saying, "Thus says my master, 'You shall eat no more of my bread, for I am estranged from you. This I give you only that you may not have it to say that I refused to give aught to my enemy when he asked of me.'" Satan took the bread, and sent back the maid with this message, "As this bread is burned and blackened, so will I make thy body; in one hour I will lay thee and thy house desolate." And I answered him, "That thou doest, do quickly; for I am ready to bear whatsoever thou canst bring upon me."

Then Satan went up straightway under the firmament of the heaven, and asked of the Lord authority over me and my possessions. And the Lord granted it to him, but not at that time.

Now I must tell you, my children, of my manner of life, and my goods that I had, before I was despoiled. I had 130,000 sheep, of which 7000 were set apart for the clothing of the fatherless, and widows, and poor; and a pack of 800 dogs guarded them. I had 9000 camels; 3000 to traffic with the cities of the earth, which I laded with good things, and sent them out among the towns and villages, and had their loads distributed to the poor. I had also 130,000 asses; 500 of them were set apart that their foals might be sold, and the price given to the poor.

Also the four gates of my house were always left open to this end, that if any poor man came to beg, and saw me sitting at one of the gates, he might not turn back abashed, but might go round to another of the gates, and enter in and receive what he needed.

Within the house also I had always thirty tables ready prepared for the entertainment of strangers, and other twelve tables appointed for the widows. None left my house with his purse empty, and whenever any came to ask help, he was constrained first of all to sit down and dine. I had fifty bakehouses, and of these, twelve served the tables of the poor.

And so it was that many strangers came to my house, and some of them desired to follow my way of life and minister to the poor, but they were in need of money to furnish them therefor. And to such men I freely lent the money, taking no security of them, but only a written acknowledgment. And sometimes they prospered in their merchandise and gained money to give to the poor; but sometimes they failed and came back to me, saying, "Have patience with us." And thereupon I would destroy the bill of their debt before them, and forgive them that which they owed me.

Sometimes also there would come to me a man of a kindly heart who would say, "I have not wherewith to help the poor, but let me wait upon them today at your table." And at evening, when he was departing, I used to say to him, "I know that you are a laboring man, and look to your wages." And so I paid him wages for the day and let him go.

I had also psalteries and a ten-stringed lute, and every day when the widows and the poor had dined I would play to them and put them in mind of God, that they should praise Him. And if ever my handmaidens murmured at the work they had to do, I took a psaltery and sang to them of the recompense of the reward. And they were comforted, and ceased from their murmuring.

As for my children, they took part every day in the ministry, and after that they gathered together in the house of their eldest brother, and feasted there. But every morning I offered up sacrifices for them, even thirty doves, fifty kids of the goats, and twelve sheep, and a choice bullock. All of these, after I had offered up prayer, I caused to be prepared for the poor, and gave to them, saying, "Take these over and above that which you have had, and pray for my children, lest they perchance have said in their hearts, 'We are the children of a wealthy father, and these goods are ours. Wherefore should we wait upon the poor and waste our substance in this manner?'" For indeed pride is an abomination unto the Lord.

Now this was my manner of life for seven years after that the angel had come to me. But when Satan had obtained from the Lord power against me, he came down in great wrath; and first he burned up the 7000 sheep, and 3000 camels, and 500 asses, and 500 yoke of oxen; and the rest were carried away by the men of the country to whom I had showed kindness, but now they turned against me and spoiled my goods. Then one came and told me, and I gave glory to God, and said not a word of complaint.

Satan therefore, when he saw how I took the matter, devised yet more against me, and took on him the likeness of the King of Persia, and came and spake to all the worthless men of the country, saying, "This man Jobab, who hath consumed all the good of the land, and left nothing, giving it away to the halt, and maimed, and blind, is the same that destroyed the temple of the great god and laid waste the place of offerings. It is time that he should receive the reward of his deeds. Come, fall upon him and spoil his house." But they said, "He hath seven sons and three daughters; what if they escape into other lands and accuse us of violence, and return and slay us?" Satan answered, "Trouble not yourselves for that. See, I have consumed part of his goods with fire; other part have I carried off. *I* will take in hand his children."

And he departed, and cast down the house upon my sons and daughters, and slew them all. And when the men saw that he had spoken truth, they came and plundered all that was in my house. Mine eyes saw worthless and dishonorable men on my couches and at my tables, and I could not utter a word, for I was stricken weak, as a sick woman. Nevertheless, I remembered the recompense of the reward; and I accounted the loss of my goods as nothing, if I might attain to that city whereof the angel had spoken.

Then there came a messenger and told me, "Thy sons and thy daughters are dead." And verily I was greatly troubled, and rent my clothes. Yet I said, "The Lord gave, and the Lord hath taken away: as it pleased the Lord, so is it come to pass: blessed be the name of the Lord."

So Satan perceived that, though all that I had possessed was taken from me, nothing could break my spirit or make me rebel against God. He departed, therefore, and asked leave of the Lord that he might afflict my body. And the Lord gave him power over my body to use it as he would, but over my life He gave him no power. Then Satan came to me as I sat upon my throne mourning for the loss of my children; and he came in the form of a great whirlwind, and cast my throne down to the ground, so that I lay for three hours without moving. And he smote me with a sore plague from head to foot, and I was filled with worms and ulcers and corruption. Therefore I arose and went out of the city in great misery and sorrow of heart, and sat upon a dunghill, being severed from the sons of men because of my evil plague. And there I remained many days. And I had no strength to work and earn my bread, so that my wife was compelled to labor as a handmaid in the house of a rich man, and carry water; and for that they gave her bread, and she brought it to me. Then was I cut to the heart, and said, "Alas for the pride of the men of this place! How can they endure to treat my wife as a slave?" Yet after that again I strengthened my soul and was patient.

After some time they refused to give my wife food enough for her and myself, but allowed her only half of what they had given her before: yet this she shared with me. Yea, she was not ashamed to go and beg of the bakers in the marketplace, that she might have wherewith to feed me.

When Satan saw her do so, he took upon him the likeness of a seller of bread. And my wife came and begged of him, supposing him to be a man; and Satan said, "Pay the price, and take what you will." But she answered, "Whence should I have money? Have you not heard of all that has befallen us? If you will show mercy, show mercy; and if not, it is your own concern." He said, "If you had not deserved misfortune, I suppose it would not have come upon you; but now, if you have no money, give me the hair of your head, and take three loaves in exchange: it may be that you can live on them for three days." And she thought within herself, "What is the hair of my head to me in comparison with the hunger of my husband?" And she said to Satan, "Come, take it." And he took a pair of shears and cut off her hair, and then gave her three loaves, in the sight of all who were in the marketplace. She took the bread and came to bring it to me, and Satan followed after her invisibly, and made her soul heavy within her. So, as she drew near to me she lifted up her voice and cried aloud, "Job, Job, how long wilt thou sit upon the dunghill waiting and expecting thy deliverance, while I wander about from house to house and labor as a slave? Behold, my sons and my daughters, whom I brought up with labor and pain, are perished and gone, and thou sittest under the open heaven filled with corruption, and I have to work day and night to get bread to keep thy soul in thy body. Lo, now have I sold the hair of my head for bread. Who would believe that I am Sitis, the wife of Job, who was clothed in fine linen woven with gold, that washed her feet in basins of silver and gold, that lay softly and was nurtured in plenty; but now I go barefoot, in rags, and sell my hair for bread. One thing only remains, for my bones are broken with very weariness of spirit. Arise and eat this bread, and satisfy thy hunger, and then speak a word against the Lord, and die; and I shall be freed from my misery and labor, and have rest."

But I answered her, "Lo, now these many years have I been set in the plague, enduring sickness of body and grief of heart, but my soul has never been so heavy in me as when I heard thee say, 'Speak a word against the

Lord, and die.' Shall we have borne the loss of our possessions, and the death of our children, and at the end lose the true riches? Remember all the good things which we enjoyed aforetime. Shall we receive those at the hands of the Lord, and not bear to receive hard things likewise? But I perceive now why thou so speakest. Come forth, thou that standest behind her to pervert her heart and make her speak as one of the foolish women. Hide thyself no longer; come forth and withstand me to the face." Then Satan came forth from behind my wife, and stood before me ashamed, and even weeping in the bitterness of his heart; and he said, "Job, thou hast prevailed: thou art flesh and I am a spirit, but I can do no more against thee." And he departed from me in confusion. And I, my children, thought of fighters whom I had seen: one had thrown the other on the ground and filled his mouth with sand, and bruised every limb of his body, yet still he kept his hold; and of a sudden the one that was uppermost could endure the grip no longer, and gave in, so that the undermost won the crown. Thus was it with me and Satan; and, my children, I counsel you to be long-suffering in all that may come upon you; for there is nothing that is stronger than patience.

Now it was not until many years had passed that the tidings of my affliction came to the ears of the kings who were of old time my friends — for Satan caused the matter to be kept from them. But when they heard, they set forth from their countries and came to visit me, even Eliphaz of Teman, and Bildad, and Zophar, and Elihu; all of them with great trains of followers. When they were come into my land they inquired, "Where is Jobab, the ruler of Uz?" And it was told them, "He sitteth upon a dunghill without the city." And they asked what was become of my wealth — for I was aforetime richer than all the princes of the East

— and they were informed of all that had befallen me.
So they came where I was, and some of the men of the
city with them, who showed me to them. But they said,
"This is not Jobab." Yet the men of the place affirmed
that it was so; and after they had disputed for some
time, Eliphaz called to me, "Art thou Jobab, our fel-
low-king?" And I, weeping and casting dust upon my
head, bowed myself in token that it was I.

Then were they stricken with great astonishment and
terror, and fell to the ground as it were dead; and they
rent their clothes and cast off their armor, and sat down
upon the ground. And Elihu lifted up his voice and
took up a lamentation over me, calling to mind all the
glory of my former state, my sheep and oxen, camels
and asses, my golden beds and my jeweled throne, the
lamps and perfumes of my palace, and the beauty of
my children, and saying, "Where is now the glory of
thy kingdom?" And when he had ended his lamentation I said, "Hold your peace and I will tell you."

"My throne is in the region beyond the world, and
the glory and beauty of it is at the right hand of the
Father.

"This world shall pass away and the glory of it shall
perish, and they that pay heed thereto shall be over-
whelmed in the overthrow of it; but my throne is in
the land of the holy, and the glory of it in the age that
hath no change.

"The rivers shall be dried up, and the abundance of
their streams floweth down into the depths of the pit;
but the rivers of my land fail not, and their streams
water it forevermore.

"Kings shall pass away, and rulers be no more seen:
their names and their boasting shall be as the image
in the glass; but my kingdom abideth forever, and the
glory thereof is as the glory of the chariot of the Most
High."

Then Eliphaz waxed very wroth, and said, "Come, and let us leave him to his folly. To what purpose have we journeyed hither to comfort him, if he rails against us and says, 'Your kingdom shall be brought to naught, but mine endureth forever'?" And he would have gone away in a rage. But Bildad restrained him, saying, "Remember that the man is sick in body and mind; we should not deal harshly with him; it may well be that he is mad." And Bildad and Zophar put questions to me to discern whether I was of sound mind or not, and I answered them soberly. And at last Zophar said, "What shall be done for thee? Behold, we have with us the most skillful physicians that are in our kingdoms. Wilt thou that they shall tend thee? Peradventure thou mayest find relief at their hands." But I said, "My healing and my medicine shall be from the Lord, who is the Maker of physicians and of all their craft."

While I was yet speaking, there came to us my wife Sitis, clothed in rags, and she had escaped by stealth out of the house of her master; for he would have kept her within, fearing that the kings would call him to account for his ill-usage of us. So when she came to us, she threw herself down before Eliphaz and said, "Rememberest thou, Eliphaz and thy fellows, how I looked and how I was attired in the former days? Look now and see in what guise I go about." And they were cut to the heart and wept, but knew not what to say; only Eliphaz took off his purple robe and put it about her shoulders. And she besought them, saying, "I pray you, command your servants to dig among the ruins of the house that fell upon our children, and seek out their bones that they may be buried and a memorial set up; for till this day we have never been able to do so because of the cost. Consider, I beseech you, what I suffer that have lost ten children, and not one of them is given to burial." So they prepared to dig; but I prevented them, and said, "Labor not in vain; ye will not find my children, for they have been taken up into the heavens by the King that created them." Again they said, "Who would not say that thou art mad? Thy children are taken up into heaven, sayest thou? Show us now what thou meanest."

I said, therefore, "Raise me up that I may stand on my feet." And they took each an arm and raised me, and I stood up and made supplication to the Father, and then said to them, "Lift up your eyes and look towards the east." And they looked, and beheld my children crowned with glory in the heavens, and above them the glory of the Most High. Which when Sitis my wife saw, she fell upon her face and worshipped, and said, "Now know I that there is remembrance of me with God. I will go now into the city and rest a little, and refresh myself for my labors of the morrow." So she went into the city, and entered into the stable of the kine that had been hers, and had been taken from her by those that employed her; and she lay down by one of the mangers and slept, having her mind at rest, and so died. And on the morrow her master sought her, and did not find her; and at last entering into the stable, he saw her lying dead there, and ran out and summoned men to him; and all the city came and saw her lying in the stable, and the beasts standing about her, lowing and making lamentation over her. Then they carried her forth and buried her beside the place of the house that had fallen upon her children.

Now as for all the words which Eliphaz, and Bildad, and Zophar, and Elihu spake with me, and those wherewith I answered them, are they not written in the book for your remembrance? Also ye know how that at the last the Lord came and answered me out of the whirlwind, and rebuked us. And we made atonement for that which we had said amiss: all but Elihu, for into him Satan had entered, and he had spoken evil words against me; wherefore he departed, and made no atonement for his sin.

Also ye know how the Lord restored to me my former state, and gave me the double of all that I had possessed before; and how I married your mother, and she bare me you: seven sons and three daughters, as it is this day.

And now behold, my sons, I die; and as for you, forget not ye the Lord, do good to the poor, pass not by the helpless, take not to yourselves wives from among the heathen.

Moreover, Job said, "I will divide my substance among you, and each of you shall possess his portion in peace."

Then Job divided his substance among his seven sons, but to his daughters he gave none of it; and they were grieved, and said, "Father, are we not also thy children?" And he answered, "Trouble not yourselves, for I have prepared for you an inheritance better than that of your brethren." And he called to him his eldest daughter, and gave her his signet-ring, saying, "Go into the treasure-chamber and bring me the three golden caskets which you will find there." And when she had brought them, he opened them, and took from them three cords, and gave one to each of his daughters. Now these cords were exceeding beautiful, of many colors, and sending forth sparks of light as it had been rays of the sun; and he said to his daughters, "Gird them about you, and keep them all the days of your life."

But Keziah, the second of the daughters, said, "Father, is this that excellent inheritance which you promised to us? What is the use of these cords? Shall we be able to live by means of them?" And he answered, "Not only so, but they will bring you even into the better life. Know ye not, my children, what is the worth of these cords? These are they which the Lord gave me on the day when He had mercy on me and healed me of my sickness; for He gave them to me, and said to me, 'Rise up, gird thy loins like a man, and I will inquire of thee and thou shalt answer Me.' And I put them about me, and straightway all my sores and plagues fell away from me, and my body was strengthened as if I had never been sick; and, moreover, I forgot all my pain and sorrow of heart. Now therefore, my children, so long as ye have these about you, the enemy can do nothing against you; no, not even to put into your minds evil thoughts. Arise, then, and gird yourselves with them before I die."

Then they did so, and their hearts were changed and renewed within them, so that they forgot the things of this world, and began to speak in the language of the angels, singing praises to the Lord of the heavens, and telling of the glory of that place and of the mighty works of the Father. And I, Nahor, the brother of Job, who wrote this testament, sat by and heard them; and that which I could I wrote down in a book, to be for them that come after, that they might know somewhat of the wonders of the Lord.

Now after three days wherein Job kept his bed — yet without pain or sickness, for no disease had power over him since the day when he put on that heavenly girdle — after three days, I say, he was aware of those that were coming to bear away his soul. And he arose, and gave to his eldest daughter a harp, and to the second a censer, and to the third an instrument of music, that they might welcome those that were on their way. And even as they took them into their hands they saw the chariots of light approaching; and they uttered hymns of praise and thanksgiving, each one in the language of them that dwell in the holy places. Then He that sat in the great chariot came near and took the soul of

Job, embracing it in His arms in the sight of his daughters; but no man else saw that sight. And He took it into the chariot and departed towards the sunrising.

And after three days we made ready the body of Job to the burial; and all the widows, and the fatherless, and the helpless came about us, crying and saying, "Woe unto us this day, woe unto us! He that was the strength of the weak, the light of the blind, the father of the fatherless, the home of the homeless, is taken from us." And they would not that his body should be hidden out of their sight. But when we carried him to the sepulcher, his three daughters went before, girded with the heavenly girdles, and giving glory to God in hymns and psalms of thanksgiving. And we laid him in the tomb as it were sleeping a fair sleep; and verily he left after him a name that shall be famous and renowned in all generations.

Solomon and the Demons

*I*n an ancient Greek book called The Testament (that is, the Last Words') of Solomon, the story is told of the way in which Solomon overcame the demons and made them serve him. The tale is put into the mouth of the king himself.

When I was engaged upon the building of the temple in Jerusalem, there was a lad, the son of the foreman of the builders, of whom I took notice, for he was a clever workman. Indeed, so skillful was he that I increased his wages and his allowance of food above the rest. Yet in spite of that, as I saw him by day, I noticed that he was becoming thin and weak and pale. So one day I called him and asked him whether anything was the matter with him. At first he would not tell me, but when I pressed him he said, "I know not whether you will believe it, O king, but a strange thing has been afflicting me. Every night when I go to my bed, something comes and sucks my right thumb, and, moreover, it steals away my food; and I feel that it is taking away all my strength, and I believe that it is an evil spirit." When I heard that, I went back to my palace, and thought earnestly, and consulted the writings of the ancients; and I prayed that a way might be shown to me how I could set the lad free from the power of the demon. And after some days there came to me an angel, and brought me a ring with a stone in it, on which was cut the figure that is called the Pentalpha and within it the Name that may not be spoken; and he told me what I must do with it. On the morrow, therefore, I sent for the lad and gave him the ring, saying, "Take this, and tonight, when the creature comes, you must cast the ring into its bosom, and say, \ In the strength of the Name, King Solomon calleth thee.' Then rise up and come running to me, and be not afraid for whatever the demon may say to you."

So that night at the accustomed hour the wicked demon Ornias came to the lad's chamber, with intent to suck his blood and take away his food. But the lad remembered my words, and cast the ring upon the demon, saying, "Come, for Solomon calleth thee," and set off at once to my palace. But the demon shrieked out after him, "Boy, what hast thou done? Take the ring from me, and I will give thee the hidden gold of the earth; take it off, and bring me not before Solomon!" But the lad took no heed; and running into the palace, he called to me, "O king, I have brought the spirit, as you told me; he is there before the door, screaming and entreating me and promising me the hidden treasures of the earth if I will not force him to come to you." Then I rose up from my throne and went out into the court of the palace, and saw the creature, in the form of a flame of fire, quivering and shrinking; and I stood over it, and said, "What is thy name?" And it answered, "Ornias." And I bade Ornias reveal to me, in the strength of the ring, how I should make him subject to me; and he told me where his abode was, and how he afflicted men, and all that I asked him. Then I sealed him with the seal of the ring, and appointed him to hew stones for the building of the temple.

Thereafter, when I had considered what I should do, I called for Ornias, and delivered the ring to him, and bade him bring before me Beelzebul, the prince of all the demons. So Ornias went to Beelzebul, and found him sitting upon his throne, and said, "Solomon calleth for thee." And Beelzebul said scornfully, "Who is this Solomon of whom thou speakest?" And Ornias cast the ring into the bosom of Beelzebul, and said again, "Solomon calleth for thee." And at that Beelzebul uttered a mighty roar, and cast forth from his mouth a great flame of fire; but he must needs rise up from his throne and follow Ornias, and stand before me. And when I saw him, I gave thanks to the Most High, who had given me power over the demons. And I spoke roughly to him; and he promised to bring before me all the demons, and that they should be subject to me, and do all that I commanded them. And I appointed him to saw blocks of marble in pieces for the work of the temple; but when the other demons saw their lord and master laboring like a slave, they shrieked aloud and were sorely dismayed.

After that I sent for many of the chief of the demons, one by one, and questioned them concerning their deeds, what diseases they sent upon men, and what secret things they knew, and how they were to be subdued; and when they had told me, I bound them, and set them to work upon the building of the temple.

Now the shapes in which they appeared before me were manifold: one was like a beautiful woman, but she had one foot like an ass's hoof; and another like a man without a head, and a flame of fire coming out of his neck; another like a great dog. These two I bound together, and the dog kept watch over the headless man, and the flame of fire that came from his neck gave light to the workmen by night. There were also dragons, one with three heads, and one with the head of a man. Another had a face that shone with a green light, and hair like serpents, but the rest of his body was darkness; and yet another was a dark man with shining eyes, and a drawn sword in his hand, who said that he was the spirit of one of the old giants who perished in the days of the flood. And of some I saw no shape, but only heard a voice. But over all of them I had dominion, and I appointed them tasks. Some I made to carry water to the builders, and some made ropes; others melted the gold and silver, and others lifted the stones. So the temple was built speedily, and I, Solomon, enjoyed great honor and peace and tranquility in my kingdom, and the kings and princes of all the regions round about came to visit me, and brought me precious gifts; and my kingdom was greatly exalted.

Now in those days, as I was sitting on my throne in the midst of my palace (and Ornias the demon was standing by me), there came before me an old man, one of my workmen, and cast himself down before me, and cried to me to do him justice against his son; for his son ill-treated him and beat him and plucked out his hair. When I heard that, I had pity on him, for he was an old man, and weak; and I sent for his son, and asked him why he dealt so with his father. But the son denied it, saying, "I am not so given over to wickedness that I should strike my father. Be it far from me, O king: I have done no such evil." I sent him away, therefore, and called his father again, and bade him be reconciled with his son; but he said, "Nay, but let him die the death." Wherefore I was perplexed, and it was in my mind to give sentence against the young man; but it happened that I looked at Ornias the demon, and I saw that he was laughing. So I sent the people away, and said to Ornias, "Accursed one, why dost thou laugh at me?" He answered, "Forgive me, O king; it was not at thee that I laughed, but at this wretched old man: because he is contriving an evil death for his son, and, lo! in three days his son will fall sick and die." Then said I, "Is this the truth?" And he said, "It is." Then I sent for the old man and his son, and said to them, "Strive to make agreement between yourselves, and after three days come again to me; and in the meantime I will send you your food from my table." And they did obeisance and departed. And when the three days were past, I saw the old man come into the judgment-hall; and he was dressed in garments of mourning, and his face was sad. I said therefore to him, "Where is thy son?" And he answered, "I have no son: this day have I carried him to his burial."

So when he was departed, I said to Ornias, "How was it that thou knewest these things?" And he answered, "It is thus, O king. We who are spirits can fly up into the air under the firmament, and we hover about among the stars and overhear the decrees that go forth from the heavens against the children of men when they are appointed to die. But we cannot abide there for long, and so we become weak, and fall like the leaves from the trees; and when men see us they say, 'Look, there is a falling star.' But they are not in truth stars that fall, since the stars have their appointed place in the heavens, like the sun and the moon; but it is we, the spirits of the air, who are in appearance like stars." And I sent Ornias away, and marveled greatly.

Again, in those days there came to me a letter from Adares the king of the Arabians, saying, "To King Solomon, greeting! We have heard of the wisdom that has been given to thee, and that thou art a compassionate man, and that thou hast power over all spirits that are in the air, or on the earth, or under the earth. Now be it known to thee that there is a destroying spirit in this land; for every day at dawn there arises a wind which blows for three hours, and it is so venomous that everyone on whom it blows dies, and it kills the cattle also. Now therefore we entreat thee in thy wisdom to devise some means, and if it may be, send us a man who can capture the spirit; and if thou canst do so, then I and my people will be tributary unto thee, and Arabia shall keep peace with thee. And, we beseech thee, make not light of our petition, for we are in a great strait. And so farewell."

When I had read this letter, I folded it up again and gave it to my chief counselor, saying, "Bring it again to my remembrance after seven days." Then I thought upon the matter; and after the seven days I called one of my servants and said to him, "Make ready a camel, and get an empty wine-skin." And he did so. Now the wine-skin was made of a whole hide of a beast, so that it had the upper parts of the four legs remaining upon it, the legs being sewn up, and the neck open. I said to him further, "Take this ring and go into Arabia, to the place where the venomous wind blows, and take the skin and hold the ring in front of the mouth of the skin towards the wind, so that the wind shall blow through the ring; and when the skin is blown up, you will know that the demon is inside it. Then hasten and tie up the neck of the skin, and seal it with the ring, and put it upon the camel, and bring it to me. But if on the way the demon promise you gold and silver and treasures to let him go, see that you do not obey him; but rather make him reveal to you where the treasures are hid, and mark the places, and come on to me. Now go, and good success be with you." So my servant set out and came to Arabia; and the men of the country doubted much whether he could capture the spirit. But when the day was dawning, even the first day after his coming, he rose up and set the skin with its mouth towards the wind, and laid the ring in the mouth of it; and the wind blew through the ring and entered into the skin and puffed it up. And the man caught the neck of the skin and closed it, and sealed it with the ring in the name of the Most High. Then he abode yet three days in the place to make trial of his success; but the poisonous wind blew no more, so that all the Arabians were assured that the demon was safely shut up. And they rejoiced greatly, and gave him many precious gifts, and did him great honor; and when he set forth to come back to me, they accompanied him to their borders. So he brought the skin back to Jerusalem, and put it in the midst of the temple.

Now at this time I, Solomon, was somewhat in the place to make trial of his success; but the poisonous wind blew no more, so that all the Arabians were assured that the demon was safely shut up. And they rejoiced greatly, and gave him many precious gifts, and did him great honor; and when he set forth to come back to me, they accompanied him to their borders. So he brought the skin back to Jerusalem, and put it in the midst of the temple.

Now at this time I, Solomon, was somewhat troubled, because I had a great stone made ready to be placed upon the corner of the temple, and none of my workmen and none of the demons were able to lift it and set it in its appointed place; but I was exceedingly desirous to put it there, because it was of such beauty and excellence. And on the morning after my servant was come back out of Arabia, I went down to the temple, thinking by what means I could lift the stone. And as I entered the temple I saw the skin; and it rose up and hopped seven paces, and fell on its face and did obeisance to me; and I marveled, and bade it stand up; and it stood on its feet, puffed up with wind. Then I asked, "Who are you?" And a voice answered me from within the skin, "I am Ephippas who dwell in Arabia." And I said, "What can you do." And it answered, "I can overturn kings' palaces, and wither the green trees of the wood, and I can move mountains." Then I said, "Are you able to move this stone, and lift it up and set it upon the corner of the temple?" And it said, "Not only can I do so, O king, but if I have the demon that is in the Red Sea to help me, I can bring up the great Pillar that is there, and set it in whatever place you command." So I said, "Lift up the corner-stone." And the skin first of all became flattened, as if the wind was gone out of it, and slipped itself under the stone; and then it blew itself out again so that the stone was lifted up upon its back, and it walked upon its stumps, bearing the stone, to the ladder, and climbed up and set the stone safely in its place upon the corner of the temple; and I was greatly rejoiced, and all Jerusalem with me.

After that I sent Ephippas to fetch to me the demon that is in the Red Sea, and commanded them to bring with them the great Pillar; and after a while I saw the Pillar being borne through the air, and was astonished at the strength of the two demons. And when I considered with myself how mighty they were, and how they could shake the whole world in a moment of time, I feared to let them go; I made therefore a circle about them in the air with my ring, and said, "Stay there!" And the demons stayed, holding the Pillar sloping between heaven and earth; and there they are to this day. And if anyone looks, he can see the Pillar sloping in the heavens, but the demons he cannot see. But when they let fall the Pillar, then will be the end of the world.*

---

* I believe that the Pillar is the Milky Way: it is certainly meant to be

Then I questioned the demon of the Red Sea and he told me how in old times he resisted Moses in Egypt, and helped Jannes and Jambres, the two wizards who fought against Moses; and how when Pharaoh followed after the children of Israel he went with him; and when the sea returned back and drowned the Egyptians, he was overtaken by it and shut up in the depths, and he remained there until Ephippas came and brought him to me.

Thus I, Solomon, had power over the spirits of the earth, and of the air, and of the water, and made them serve me; and my kingdom was exalted, and there was peace in my days. But when I became mighty my heart was lifted up, and I committed foolishness; for I saw the daughter of a certain Jebusite, and loved her exceedingly, and asked for her in marriage. But her kinsfolk said, "You shall not take her to be your wife except you worship our gods, even the great gods Remphan and Moloch." Then I said, "I cannot worship strange gods; why would you that I should do this?" They said, "Because they are the gods of our fathers." And I refused. Then I went to the maiden and entreated her; and she also said, "I will not hearken to you, except you worship my gods." So I departed from her. But after a little, she sent me five locusts by the hand of a messenger, saying, "Take these five locusts and crush them in the name of the god Moloch, and I will be your wife." And I did so. And forthwith my glory departed from me, and I forgot my wisdom, and became weak and foolish in my mind; and the heathen woman compelled me to build temples to the false gods, to Baal, and Remphan, and Moloch; and my spirit was darkened within me, and I became a byword among men and demons.

---

one of the constellations.

Therefore have I written this testament, that men might remember me, and think of their latter end as well as of their beginning.

The Story of Ebedmelech the Ethiopian, and of the Death of Jeremiah

*W*hen the time was come when it was ordained that Jerusalem should be laid waste by the king of the Chaldeans, God spake to Jeremiah the prophet, saying, "Depart out of this city, for I am about to destroy it for the wickedness of them that dwell therein." But Jeremiah answered, "Suffer me, I beseech thee, Lord, to speak a word." And He said, "Say on." And Jeremiah said, "Wilt Thou indeed deliver Thy chosen city into the hand of the Chaldeans, that their king may boast himself against it and say, 'I have prevailed against the Holy City of God'? Not so, Lord; but if it be Thy will to destroy it, overthrow it rather with Thine own hand." And He said, "Neither the king nor his power shall prevail to destroy it, unless I first open the gates thereof to him. Come therefore at the sixth hour of the night to the city wall, thou and Baruch the scribe, and I will show you what I will do." Jeremiah therefore rent his clothes and put ashes upon his head, and went and found Baruch in the temple; and when Baruch saw him he was dismayed, and cried out, "What is the matter?" And when Jeremiah had told him that which was proposed concerning the city, he also rent his clothes; and they remained both of them in the holy place all that day weeping.

But at the sixth hour of the night they went out and walked upon the city wall. And suddenly they heard the sound of a trumpet in heaven, and there came down angels bearing torches of fire in their hands, and alighted upon the four corners of the wall of the city. Then Jeremiah and Baruch perceived that the desolation of Jerusalem was indeed at hand; and Jeremiah cried out to the angels, "I beseech you, destroy not the city until I have spoken a word to the Most High." So the angels stayed their hand; and Jeremiah said, "Lord, now we know of a truth that the city will be delivered into the hands of the Chaldeans; tell us, therefore, what wilt Thou that we shall do with the holy vessels of the temple?" And he answered, "Commit them to the earth, and say unto it, 'Hear, O earth, the voice of Him that separated thee from among the waters, and sealed thee with seven seals unto seven ages, even until the time wherein thou shalt be renewed in beauty: keep these vessels of the sanctuary until the coming of the Beloved.'" And Jeremiah continued and said, "I beseech Thee, show me what I shall do for Ebedmelech the Ethiopian, because he showed me great kindness and delivered me out of the pit wherein Zedekiah cast me; and I would not have him see the desolation of the city, for it would grieve him to the heart." The Lord said, "Send him to the vineyard of Agrippa which is on the other side of the hill, and I will shelter him until I bring back the people to the city. And as for thee, go thou with thy people to Babylon, and remain

there to comfort them until they return hither. And
let Baruch abide here until I send him word."

Then he commanded the angels, and they brake
down the corners of the wall and loosened the foun-
dations, and made weak the fastenings of the gates; and
after that a great voice sounded out of the temple,
saying, "Enter, ye enemies, and come in, ye adversaries;
for He that kept the house hath departed from it." And
the angels went up again into heaven. But Jeremiah
and Baruch went into the temple, and took the vessels
of the sanctuary and delivered them to the earth, as
they were commanded; and forthwith the earth opened
her mouth and swallowed them up. And for the rest
of that night they wept and lamented; and in the
morning Jeremiah called for Ebedmelech and said to
him, "Take a basket and go to the vineyard of Agrippa,
and fetch me some figs, that I may give them to the
sick and needy among the people; and the blessing of
God go with thee." And Ebedmelech set forth.

On that same morning the host of the Chaldeans
surrounded the city, and a trumpet sounded in heaven,
and they came against the city; and the gates gave way
before them, and the wall fell, and they entered the city
and laid it desolate, and took the people captive. But
Jeremiah took the keys of the temple, and went outside
the city and threw them up towards the sun, saying,
"O sun, I say unto thee, take these keys and keep them
until God shall require them of thee; for we are not
found worthy to keep them any longer." And they
vanished out of his sight. Then he returned, and the
Chaldeans took him prisoner and carried him away to
Babylon. But Baruch fled, and took refuge in a tomb,
and there he remained in great sorrow of heart.

Now Ebedmelech had gathered the figs, and filled
his basket; and by the time he had finished, the day
had become burning hot. So he sat him down under

a tree to rest a little, and then laid his head on the basket of figs and fell into a slumber. And he slept for sixty-six years without waking.

And when the sixty-six years were over, and the time of deliverance of the children of Israel was near, Ebedmelech woke up, and said to himself, "I should have been glad to sleep a little longer, for my head is still heavy; I have not slept my sleep out." And he uncovered his basket and looked at the figs, and saw that they were oozing with juice; and said again, "Well, I should like to sleep yet a little, but I am afraid I may oversleep myself; and if I do, father Jeremiah will be disappointed; for if he had not been in haste for the figs, he would not have sent me out so early." So he rose and picked up his basket of figs and put it on his shoulder, and went back to Jerusalem. When he came near the city he could not recognize it, and when he had entered the gate he could not either find his own house or see any of his acquaintance. He said therefore within himself, "Some strange delusion has come upon me; I have missed my way in coming over the hills: it must be that I was not fully awake. This will be a wonderful thing to tell Jeremiah when I meet with him." And he went out of the city. But when he looked back upon it, he could see that it was indeed Jerusalem; and he said, "It is surely the city, yet there is something wrong." He went into the city the second time, but he could find none that knew him. And he said, "God preserve me! Verily a delusion has fallen upon me," and went outside the city and sat down with the basket of figs, saying, "Here will I sit until my eyes are opened, and I can discern the truth." After some time he saw an old man coming from the fields, and said to him, "Old man, what is this city, I pray you?" The old man said, "It is Jerusalem." Ebedmelech said, "Where are Jeremiah the prophet and Baruch the scribe?" The old man answered, "You are certainly not of this city, that you inquire concerning these men. Jeremiah is in Babylon with the people that were carried away captive by Nebuchadnezzar the king." Then Ebedmelech marveled and said, "If you were not an aged man, whom it is not lawful to mock, I should have said you were mad. How many hours is it, think you, since Jeremiah sent me to the garden of Agrippa for some figs for the sick people, and I went and gathered them and slumbered for a little under a tree, and have just now brought them back; and here they are with the juice oozing from them, just as when I picked them; and you say the people and Jeremiah are gone to Babylon!" And he opened the basket and showed the figs. And when the old man saw them he said, "Verily, my son, God has had mercy on you. He has spared you from seeing the desolation of the city. Behold, today it is sixty-and-six years since the people were carried away. And, if you believe not me, look upon the trees and see that it is not the time of figs." Then Ebedmelech asked, "What then is this month, and what is the day?" And he answered, "It is the twelfth day of Nisan." And Ebedmelech believed, and gave thanks to God; and after that he gave the old man some of the figs, and bade him farewell, saying, "May God guide thee to the Jerusalem which is above." And he went to find Baruch.

And after a while he found him dwelling in a tomb; and they greeted one another, and rejoiced, and Ebedmelech told Baruch all that had happened to him, and Baruch marveled and praised God. Then they consulted how they might send word to Jeremiah at Babylon; for they perceived that the time of the return of Israel was at hand. And it was revealed to them that on the morrow at dawn there should come a messenger whom they might send.

On the morrow, therefore, Baruch rose early and went out of the tomb, and saw an eagle sitting upon a rock hard by; and he called to it and it came, and spoke with a man's voice, saying, "I am sent hither to bear a message for thee." Baruch said, "Canst thou carry a letter to Babylon, to Jeremiah the prophet?" And the eagle said, "To that end am I sent." So they wrote a letter, and took fifteen of the figs from the basket and hung them on the eagle's neck; and Baruch blessed it, saying, "I say unto thee, O king of the birds, go in peace, and bring back an answer to me. Be not like the raven, which Noah sent out, and it returned no more to the ark; but be like the dove, which returned the third day with an answer of peace. And if the birds of the air come against thee, fight with them, and the power of God be with thee. Turn neither to the right hand nor to the left, but go straight as an arrow in the strength of the Most High."

Then the eagle flew and rested not till it came to Babylon; and there it perched upon a tree in a desert place outside the city, and waited until Jeremiah and some of the people passed by, carrying a dead man to burial. And it rose up and lighted upon the bier of the dead man, and he revived. And the eagle said to Jeremiah, "Gather the people together, and take the letter which is upon my neck, and read it in their ears." And he did so; and the people rejoiced, because the time of their deliverance was at hand. Then Jeremiah wrote a letter to Baruch, and put it upon the eagle's neck. And he blessed the eagle, and sent it away; but the figs he gave to the sick among the people. And the eagle returned to Jerusalem, and gave the letter to Baruch; and when he read it he wept, because Jeremiah had written in it all the afflictions which the people suffered at the hands of the Chaldeans.

Now when the time was fulfilled, the people were set free from Babylon, and returned to Jerusalem. And when they came back, they rejoiced and gave thanks for their deliverance for nine days. And on the tenth day Jeremiah stood up before all of them and sang a hymn of praise; and when he had ended it, he fell on the ground and became as one dead. When they saw that, Baruch and Ebed-melech lifted up their voices and wept, saying, "Our father Jeremiah, the priest of God, is departed from us!" And all the people ran together and saw Jeremiah lying as dead; and they rent their clothes and bewailed him, and then made ready to bury him. But there came a voice, saying, "Bury not the living." And at that they left off preparing a sepulcher for him, and waited, keeping watch about his body, till he should revive again.

And after three days the spirit of Jeremiah returned to him again, and he rose up and prophesied; and in his prophecy he said, "There shall be a Tree set up, which shall make the barren trees fruitful, and the proud and fruitful trees barren; and the snow shall be turned to blackness, and the sweet waters become bitter, and the scarlet shall be white as wool. Moreover, He shall bless the isles that they shall bear fruit by the word of His mouth; and He shall satisfy the hungry souls." And thereafter he began to speak to them of the coming of the Beloved into the world.

Now when the people heard it they were very angry and said, "He blasphemeth. These are the words that Isaiah spake, and they sawed him asunder with a saw of wood. Let us slay Jeremiah also, but him we will stone with stones." And Baruch and Ebedmelech cried out against them, "Do not this great wickedness!" But Jeremiah said, "Be silent, for they shall not kill me before I have delivered to you all that I have seen and heard. Fetch me a great stone." And when it was brought, Jeremiah prayed and said, "O Light of the Ages, cause this stone to appear in my likeness." And immediately the stone took upon it the likeness of Jeremiah, and the people began to stone it, believing that it was Jeremiah. And in the meantime he went on speaking to Baruch and Ebedmelech until he had committed to them all the mysteries which he had heard while he lay in a trance.

Then he arose and stood forth in the midst of the people, and the stone cried out with a loud voice, "O foolish people, why stone ye me, thinking that I am Jeremiah; and behold, he is in the midst of you!" And their eyes were opened, and they ran upon him and stoned him; and his ministry was accomplished.

But Baruch and Ebedmelech buried his body; and they took the stone and set it up over his grave, and wrote upon it, "This is the helper of Jeremiah."

Ahikar

I

*I*n the Book of Tobit in the Apocrypha you will find
mention in several places of a man called Achiacharus,
who was a relation of Tobit, In the first chapter (verses
21, 22) you read that he was a great officer at the court
of king Esarhaddon; and at the end of the book (xiv.
10) you may learn something about his story; for Tobit
says to his son Tobias, "Remember, my son, how Aman
handled Achiacharus that brought him up, how out
of light he brought him into darkness, and how he
rewarded him again; yet Achiacharus was saved, but
the other had his reward, for he went down into darkness," Then it goes on, "Manasses gave alms, and
escaped the snare that was set for him, but Aman fell
into the snare and perished."

Now of late years the book has come to light which
tells the whole history of Achiacharus (or Ahikar, as
we shall call him), and you will see as you go on that
in the Book of Tobit some mistakes have been made
in the names, and that instead of Aman we shall have
to read Nadan, and instead of Manasses, Achiacharus.

This is the story of Ahikar. He is made to tell it himself, and he says:

When I was a young man I was steward to the great king Esarhaddon, the king of Nineveh. I was rich, and had great estates and beautiful palaces; I had everything that my heart desired, except one thing: and that was, a son. I had no child to comfort me and to inherit my great possessions after me.

Many times did I go to the temples of the gods of Nineveh and offer them sacrifices and gifts and burn incense before them; and I said, "O gods, give me a son, that I may enjoy his company while I live, and when I die he may close my eyes and bury me. And verily I am so rich that if every day from the day of my death until he died he were to take a bushel of my money and cast it away, he would not come to the end of it before his death." But the gods of Nineveh made me no answer.

Then I bethought me of the God of Israel, of whom I had learned when I was a child (for I came out of the land of the Hebrews), and I turned to Him and besought Him in like manner that He would grant me a son. And a voice came to me saying, "Forasmuch as thou hast put thy trust in false gods and sacrificed to them, thou shalt have no son. Yet this do: take thy sister's son Nadan, who is a young child, and bring him up as thine own son."

So I took Nadan and gave him to eight nurses to bring him up. He was fed on all manner of dainties, he was clothed in purple and scarlet, and slept on the softest beds. He grew up like a fair young cedar tree; and I instructed him in all my wisdom, until I was sixty years old.

One day the king Esarhaddon returned from journeying through his kingdom, and sent for me and said, "Ahikar, my friend, my faithful and wise counselor, you are becoming an old man. If you die, who shall succeed you and serve me in your place?" I answered, "O king, live forever. There is with me the son of my sister, whom I have brought up as my own son, and have instructed him in all the ways of wisdom." The king said, "Go, bring him before me, and if I take pleasure in him, he shall serve me in your stead, and you can have rest from your labors, and joy and honor in your old age." So I brought Nadan to the king; and when the king saw him, he delighted in him and said, "The gods preserve you, my son!" And to me he said, "As you have served me and my father Sennacherib, so shall this youth serve me, and I will honor him and promote him for your sake." And I gave thanks to the king, and we went out, I and Nadan, from his presence. And I took Nadan home and spoke to him in private, telling him how he should conduct himself, and of what men he ought to beware, and whom he should trust. All these precepts are written in the book of Ahikar, but they are not put down here.

Now I hoped that Nadan would pay heed to my words of instruction; but when the king had exalted him, and taken him to live at the palace with him, I was grieved to see that Nadan began to become wasteful and unruly, and that, if I had suffered him, he would have squandered my money and ill-treated my servants. I admonished him, therefore, but it was in vain. He said, "My uncle Ahikar is getting old and timorous: his wisdom is failing him: one need not pay much heed to what he says." And by degrees I saw that the king began to believe Nadan, and that he no longer received me with such honor as in the old days: and this was a grief to me.

Now as I no longer had Nadan to live with me, I considered, and took his younger brother Nabu-zardan into my house. But when Nadan heard of this, he was very angry, for he thought, "Is this old man going to leave all his possessions to my younger brother, and turn me out?" So he began to think and plot how he might put me out of the way, and himself gain favor with the king.

And at last he sat down and wrote certain letters. In the first he deceitfully imitated my handwriting, and sealed it with my seal. It was written in my name to the king of Persia, saying, "From Ahikar, scribe and treasurer to Esar-haddon, king of Assyria, greeting! As soon as thou hast received this letter, set forth with thine host, and come to the plain of the south, on the 25th day of this month, and I will guide thee to Nineveh, and thou shalt take the city and possess the kingdom without any strife or battle." This letter he left lying in my chamber in the palace.

The other was written to me in the king's name, and sealed with his seal, "To Ahikar from Esarhaddon, greeting! As soon as thou receivest this letter, assemble the army, and go to the plain of the south, on the 25th day of this month; and when thou shalt see me, range the troops as if for battle, and come quickly towards me: for I have the ambassadors of the king of Egypt with me, and I desire that they should see the might of my army." This letter Nadan sent to me, and I began to make preparations as it commanded me. Thereafter Nadan took the first letter, feigning to have found it in my chamber, and brought it to king Esarhaddon. And when the king had read it, he was very angry and said, "O ye gods! what have I done to Ahikar that he should seek to betray me thus?" Nadan said, "Perhaps, my lord, it is a forgery; be not too soon disturbed; let us wait till the day appointed, and then go to the plain of the south; if Ahikar is not there, we shall know that the letter is not his; but if he is there, and armed men with him, I fear that he must indeed be conspiring against thee." And the king consented.

On the twenty-fifth day of the month, therefore, the king and Nadan set forth and rode out to the plain of the south. And I, as I had been commanded, was there with the great army which I had gathered; and so soon as I saw the king and his train approaching, I drew up the soldiers in battle array and marched quickly towards him, and the soldiers waved their weapons and shouted, and there was a great noise. Then the king was very sorely troubled, for he was sure that I had rebelled against him. But Nadan said, "Go back, my lord king, to the palace; I will capture that evil old man and bring him before you." And the king departed with his servants.

But Nadan rode up to me and said, "All that you have done is right, and well performed; the king is greatly pleased with you, and desires that you will send away the soldiers to their homes and come before him alone to receive your reward." So we rode into the city, and he brought me into the palace, where the king was seated on his throne, and all his servants about him; and I perceived that the king was in displeasure, but I knew not why. Then he put into my hand the letter which was written in my name to the king of Persia, and said, "Read that letter." And when I had read it, my knees knocked against each other, and I was speechless; I sought for a word of wisdom, but I found none. Nadan cried aloud, "O wicked and foolish old man, come forth from the presence of the king; stretch out thy hands for the cords and thy feet for the fetters!" And they bound me.

Then the king Esarhaddon turned away his face from me and spoke to Nabushemak, the chief of the executioners, who had been my friend, and said, "Take Ahikar, smite off his head, and remove it a hundred ells from his body." And I fell on my face and said, "O king, live forever! It is thy will to slay me, yet I know that I have not sinned against thee. Now, my lord, I beseech thee, command that I may be slain before the door of my own house, and that my body may be given to my wife to be buried." And the king gave commandment accordingly.

Now as they were taking me to my house, I sent a messenger before me to my wife Ashfagni, who was a very wise woman. And she, when she heard what had happened, did not waste time in making lamentation, but hastened and prepared refreshment for Nabushemak and for the slaves that were his helpers. She came forth to meet them, and accompanied them into the house, and set food and wine before them; and the slaves drank of the wine till they were drunken and fell into a deep sleep, everyone in his place.

Then I said to Nabushemak, "Do you remember how, when the father of the king delivered you to me to be put to death, I spared you because I knew that you had not done that for which you were condemned; and how, when the king learned that you were guiltless, he took you into favor again, and rewarded me? Now I swear to you that I likewise have not conspired against king Esarhaddon, but I have been falsely accused. Save me therefore; but lest the rumor should be spread abroad that I have not been put to death, do this. I have a prisoner in my house who is condemned justly to death. Take my clothes and put them upon him, and smite off his head; behold, your servants are drunken and will perceive nothing, and I will be in hiding until the day when the truth is made known."

And Nabushemak was glad — for he was my friend — and agreed; and it was done as I advised. The slaves took the prisoner and smote off his head, perceiving nothing, and gave his body to be buried instead of me;

and it was published throughout all Nineveh and Assyria that Ahikar was dead.

Then Nabushemak and my wife Ashfagni made a hiding place in the ground; it was four cubits long and three broad and five in height, and it was covered with a stone. There they hid me, and gave me bread and water to eat, secretly, and there I abode many days. But Esarhaddon was grieved in spirit, and said to Nadan, "Go to the house of Ahikar and celebrate his funeral, for he was thy uncle, and served me and my father faithfully for a long time." So Nadan came to my house; but he did not celebrate my funeral. He gathered together strange men and women, and feasted with them, and sang, and drank, and was drunken. He mocked at my wife Ashfagni, and as for my servants, who loved me and had been long in my house, he stripped them and beat them and ill-treated them until I heard the voice of their weeping and crying in my hiding place, and I prayed the Most High to deliver us and to reward Nadan according to his works.

II

*N*ow when Pharaoh, king of Egypt, heard that I, Ahikar, was dead, he was very glad; for he had always stood in awe of my wisdom. And he wrote a letter to Esarhaddon in these words: "Pharaoh, king of Egypt, to Esarhaddon, king of Assyria, greeting! I desire to build a castle between heaven and earth. Send me therefore a wise man to whom I may commit the business. If he accomplishes all that I require and answers all my questions, I will send you by his hands the whole revenue of Egypt for three years. But if you cannot send me such a man, then you must send to me, by my messenger, the whole revenue of Assyria for three years. And if not, I shall come against you and lay your land desolate. And so farewell."

When the letter was read before Esarhaddon, he called together his princes and counselors and wise men, and said to them, "Which of you will go to Egypt and answer the questions of Pharaoh?" They said, "Lord and king, in the time of your father it was Ahikar the scribe who answered all hard questions and solved all difficulties; and behold, now you have with you his sister's son Nadan, who has been instructed in his wisdom and can do all that you require." So the king turned to Nadan and said, "Will you go to Egypt and answer Pharaoh?" But Nadan said, "It is folly! The gods themselves could not build a castle between heaven and earth; how then should the children of men accomplish such a thing?" When the king heard that, he arose and came down from his throne, and threw himself on the ground lamenting and saying, "Alas, alas, I am undone. I have slain my servant Ahikar at the word of a foolish boy, and there is none like him left! Who can give him back to me?"

Then Nabushemak spoke and said, "O king, live forever. He that disobeys the commandments of his master is worthy of death. Say therefore the word, and let them hang me on a tree; for Ahikar, whom you bade me slay, is not dead, but living!" The king said, "O Nabushemak, if it be as you say, and if you can show me Ahikar alive, I will give you ten thousand talents of gold and a hundred robes of purple. Say on, therefore." Nabushemak said, "One thing I ask of my lord:

that he will not keep this my trespass in mind, nor store up wrath against me." And the king sware to him.

Nabushemak went forth immediately and mounted his chariot, and drove swiftly to my house. He uncovered the hiding place and brought me forth, and took me up into his chariot and led me into the presence of the king. And when the king saw me, he wept; for I was in evil plight. My hair was grown over my shoulders, and my beard reached down to my girdle; my body was foul with dirt, and my nails were as long as eagles' claws; my eyes were dim from the darkness, and my limbs were stiff so that I could scarcely walk. And the king said, "O Ahikar, it is not I that have brought this misery upon you, but he whom you have brought up as your own son." I answered, "O king, since mine eyes have looked upon you I have no more sorrow or pain." The king said, "Go to your house, bathe your body, and cut your hair; refresh yourself and take your rest for forty days; then come back to me." And I did so. But after twenty days I had recovered my strength, and I went back to the king. Then he showed me the letter of the king of Egypt, saying, "Behold, Ahikar, the burden which they would lay upon me and upon my kingdom." And I answered, "O king, live forever. Trouble not yourself, nor be disquieted about this matter. I will go to Egypt and answer the hard questions; and I will bring back to you the revenues of Egypt for three years." So the king was comforted; he rejoiced greatly, and made a feast, and gave me rich presents.

Immediately after this, I began to make ready for my journey; and first I ordered my huntsmen to catch two young eagles alive. I also chose from among my servants two young boys whose names were Nabuchal and Tabshalom, and taught them to ride upon the backs of the eagles; and after a while the eagles became accustomed to bear them up in the air. I also taught them certain words which they should say at the appointed time, and practiced them until they knew perfectly what they had to do.

And when all was prepared, I set forth with a great company and went to Egypt. It was told Pharaoh that an embassy was come from Nineveh, and he sent for me, and when I appeared before him he asked who I was. And I answered, "I am Abikam, one of the least of the servants of Esar-haddon." Pharaoh was displeased, and said, "Am I then so much despised by your master that he sends me the least of his servants?" I said, "My lord Esarhaddon is so far exalted above his servants that in his sight the great and the small are all alike." He said, "Depart from my presence, and tomorrow come again to me."

Then Pharaoh, who desired foolishly to make himself appear great in our eyes, arrayed himself in purple, and made his nobles put on scarlet and stand about him; and when I came into his presence he asked me to what I compared him. I said, "My lord, you are like the god Bel, and your nobles are like his priests." And in like manner on the following days he dressed himself in various colors, and each day asked me what I should liken him to. And I said, "To the sun" on one day, and "To the moon" on the next, and on the third day, "To the spring and the flowers of it." And he was greatly pleased, and said, "Abikam, you have compared me to the god Bel, and to the sun and the moon and the spring; now tell me, to what do you liken your master Esarhaddon?" I said, "I cannot tell you, O king, until you have risen from your throne." So Pharaoh stood up, and I said, "My lord Esarhaddon is like the great God of Heaven in respect of you: He has dominion over the god Bel, He can forbid the sun to shine and the moon to rise, and He can lay waste the spring

and all the flowers thereof." Then Pharaoh was dis-
pleased and said, "I adjure you by the life of your lord
Esarhaddon, tell me, what is your name, in very deed?"
I answered, "I am Ahikar the scribe, and the seal of
Esarhaddon is in my keeping."

Pharaoh was troubled when he learned that I was yet
alive, and he sent me away, saying, "Tomorrow come
to me and tell me a thing which neither I nor my
nobles have ever heard." So I took thought, and wrote
in the name of Pharaoh a bond in which it was said
that he owed to my lord Esarhaddon nine hundred
talents of gold. And next day I brought it before
Pharaoh; but before I had opened it the nobles cried
out, saying, "We know it of old, we know it well!" Then
said I, "I thank you for acknowledging the debt." And
I gave the paper to the king, and he looked on it and
said to them, "What! Do you acknowledge that I owe
nine hundred talents of gold to Esarhaddon?" And
they were confounded, and cried out again, "No! no!
we have never heard of any such thing." So I said, "If
it be so, I have done what you required."

But Pharaoh said, "It is enough: I have sent for you
to build me a castle between the earth and the heavens;
even a thousand cubits above the earth. Come forth
into the plain tomorrow and accomplish this." And I
said, "Well, O king; and do you for your part bring
masons and that which is necessary for building." So
on the morrow a great multitude assembled to see how
the matter would go. But I had my eagles and my boys
in readiness; and when Pharaoh gave the word, I sent
them up, the boys riding on the eagles; and when they
were high up in the air, the boys called out, as I had
taught them, "Bring us mortar, lime, and stones: we
are ready to begin the building!" And the masons and
all the people were amazed, gaping at the boys. And I
fell upon the masons and beat them, saying, "Why

delay you? Make haste, give them what they ask for," and suchlike words, till they fled before me. And I said to Pharaoh, "If your people refuse to do their part, how can I do mine?" And Pharaoh and his nobles murmured, but they could not think of any answer. So Pharaoh said, "It is enough; leave the matter of the castle; I have other questions to ask you."

On the morrow he called for me, and said, "I saw a great pillar built of 8763 bricks, and about it are planted twelve cedars, and each has thirty branches, and on each branch are a black and a white mouse which gnaw it." I laughed and made answer, "O king, there is not a child in the land of Assyria who could not interpret this riddle. The pillar is the year, the bricks are the hours, the cedars the months, their branches the days, and the black and white mice are the night and the day."

Pharaoh's face fell, and he said, "Well. But now I command you to plait me a rope out of the sand." I answered, "Let them bring me a pattern out of your store-house, O king, that I may have it to copy." He said, "You trifle with me; and unless you plait me such a rope I will not pay you the revenues of Egypt." I went aside therefore and considered; and knowing that the Egyptians were foolish, I thought upon a plan. I got a mass of sand and put it in a chest, and made it run out through two pipes so that when the sun shone upon it, it appeared like the strands of a rope; and I called to the king, "Let your servants plait together the two strands of the rope which I have made, and when they have done so I will make more." And again they were dismayed, and could say nothing.

Lastly, Pharaoh showed me a millstone which was broken in two pieces, and said, "Come, Ahikar, sew this together for me." But I took a small piece of a like stone, and said, "O king, I have not my tools with me;

but command your shoemaker to cut me a thread out of this piece of stone, and I will sew the millstone together forthwith." Then Pharaoh laughed, and said, "Well, Ahikar, it was on a good day for your lord that you were born. Come, I will make you a feast, and after that you shall return to your own land."

So after certain days I departed, taking with me the revenues of Egypt for three years, and also the nine hundred talents which I had made Pharaoh acknowledge that he owed to my lord. And Esar-haddon came forth to meet me; and when he heard what I had done, he made me sit down on his right hand, and said, "Ahikar, ask what thou wilt and I will give it thee." Then I said, "O king, live forever! Two things only will I require of thee: one, that thou wouldst do good unto Nabushemak, for it is by his means that I was saved alive; and the other, that thou wouldst give me power over my sister's son Nadan, and not require his life at my hand." And the king granted my request, and exalted Nabushemak to the first rank in his kingdom; but Nadan he delivered into my hand.

I took Nadan to the hall of my house, and set him with his feet in the stocks, and a collar of iron about his neck, and iron bands upon his hands; I fed him with bread and water, and chastised him with rods. And when I came in or out of my house I stood and reproached him, speaking in parables and proverbs.

Now these are some of the parables which I spake to Nadan:

"My son, thou art like one that shot an arrow into the heaven to slay God: the arrow fell back upon him and pierced him."

"Thou art like one that saw his neighbor shivering with cold, and took a vessel of cold water and poured it over him."

"Thou didst think to take my place after my death; but know that even if the tail of the pig grew seven cubits long, no man would mistake the pig for a horse."

"Thou art like the trap that was set on a dunghill. The sparrow saw it and said, 'Brother, what dost thou here?' The trap answered, 'I am fasting and praying.' The sparrow said, 'And what is that piece of wood by thee?' The trap said, 'My staff upon which I lean when I pray.' 'And what is that in thy mouth?' 'It is a little food for hungry wayfarers.' Then said the sparrow, 'I am hungry and a wayfarer.' 'Come hither then,' said the trap, 'and fear nothing.' But when the sparrow came, the trap caught it by the head; and the sparrow said, 'If these be thy fastings and prayers, God will not accept thy fasting nor hearken to thy prayer.'"

"Thou art like the pig that went to the bath along with the nobles; and when it had bathed and come forth, it saw a pool of mud, and went and rolled therein."

"Hearken: a serpent was sleeping on a thorn-bush, and a flood came and swept them both away. And a wolf saw them floating on the water, and said, 'There goes one evil upon another evil, and a third evil carrying them off.' The serpent said, 'And dost thou bring back the kids and lambs to their mothers?' 'Nay,' said the wolf. The serpent said, 'I know not whether there is much to choose betwixt us.'"

"Thou art like the mole that came up out of the ground to curse God because He had not given to it sharpness of sight; and the eagle saw it, and carried it off."

"When men say to the wolf, 'Get away from the flock,' he saith, 'Nay, but the dust thereof is healing to mine eyes.' When they took him to the school, the teacher said, 'Say A.' The wolf said, 'Lamb.' 'Say B.' He answered, 'Kid.' Surely he spake of that which was in his thoughts."

At last, after many days, Nadan besought me, saying, "Have mercy on me, spare my life, and I will feed thy swine and keep thine asses, and be thy slave forever."

And I said, "Thou art like the palm tree which bare no dates, and the owner came to cut it down; and it said, 'Leave me this one year, and next year I will bear melons.' But he said, 'Thou that hast not borne thine own fruit, how wilt thou bear one that is not thine?' Now, behold, I will say no more to thee, O Nadan; but let God, who preserved me alive, judge between thee and me."

And forthwith judgment went forth against Nadan, and his body swelled up and burst, and he died. For it is written, "He that diggeth a pit for another shall fall into the midst of it himself."

THE END